W9-BHE-307

A Room for Cathy

By CATHERINE WOOLLEY

Illustrated by Veronica Reed

SCHOLASTIC BOOK SERVICES

New York Toronto London Auckland Sydney

Copyright © 1956 by Catherine Woolley. This edition is
published by Scholastic Book Services, a division of
Scholastic Magazines, Inc., by arrangement with William
Morrow & Company.

8th printing..........................January 1970
Printed in the U.S.A.

CONTENTS

Other books by Catherine Woolley

THE ANIMAL TRAIN AND OTHER STORIES
DAVID'S CAMPAIGN BUTTONS
DAVID'S HUNDRED DOLLARS
DAVID'S RAILROAD
ELLIE'S PROBLEM DOG
GINNIE AND GENEVA
GINNIE AND THE MYSTERY HOUSE
*GINNIE AND THE NEW GIRL
GINNIE JOINS IN
HOLIDAY ON WHEELS
LUNCH FOR LENNIE
MISS CATHY LEONARD
RAILROAD COWBOY
SCHOOLROOM ZOO
TWO HUNDRED PENNIES

*A TAB Book

CHAPTER 1

No Privacy for Cathy

CATHY PAUSED at the walk leading into the Greenacres Garden Apartments. "Come in for a while, Judy," she said to her friend. "I'll show you the beautiful dress my mother gave me to dress up in. Besides," she urged, as Judy hesitated, "I won't be around here much longer."

Judy turned with her into the red-brick walk. "Are you going to move real soon?"

"We had the closing last Saturday. I'll tell you all about our new house!"

They went up two steps to the green door which led directly to the Leonards' apartment in the attractive colonial structure. Through the solid door came a series of high-pitched squeals. "That's Jeffy," Cathy said, pressing the bell. "He's being a truck, as usual."

Cathy's mother opened the door. "Hello, dear. Hello, Judy, it's nice to see you." Mrs. Leonard smiled at them. "Hang your coats in the closet, Cathy, please. I'll go stark, raving mad if anything else is dumped in this room! Where's Chris?"

"We waited for her, but a girl in her class said she was helping the teacher." Cathy shrugged out of her winter coat. The enveloping warmth in the apartment felt wonderful after the raw dampness of the January afternoon.

1

The living room was, indeed, fully occupied. An ironing board stood in the center. A clothesbasket held an assortment of dampened bundles, and several freshly pressed dresses belonging to Cathy and her younger sister Chris were spread out on chairs. Trucks of assorted sizes lay strewn about the floor. Five-year-old Jeffrey, going through a shy stage just now, had scrambled behind a chair, but he continued his truck noises, pretending not to see the girls. Only his dungaree-clad rear and the clean blond back of his little head were visible.

"May we get something to eat?" Cathy asked.

"You may." Mother preceded the two girls into the

tiny kitchen and opened the refrigerator. "Here's plenty of milk. Would you like to open a box of Girl Scout cookies?" She got down glasses and paper napkins. "You help yourselves. I want to get this ironing out of the way."

Cathy poured the milk, and she and Judy helped themselves to a liberal supply of cookies. "Let's take them into my room," Cathy said, picking up her glass and the cookie box and leading the way.

The room which Cathy and Chris shared held a double-decker bed. There would not have been room for twin beds placed side by side; as it was, a bureau, a small table, and two straight chairs took up the space. A small set of drawers at the foot of the bed, covered with gaily flowered paper, held Jeffy's socks, shorts, and jerseys, for Jeffy slept on the studio couch in the living room and there was no other place to keep his clothes.

Cathy set her refreshments on the table, then went over and closed the door. "There," she said with a sigh of contentment, slipping into a chair. Not that they had anything especially private to talk about, but in the Leonard apartment being by one's self was a rare and fleeting experience. Cathy meant to savor to the full these few minutes with Judy. She knew very well that the minutes were numbered.

They had barely nibbled a cookie when they heard the doorbell. Cathy gave an exclamation of annoyance. "That's Chris. Now she'll be in here."

"This is an awfully little apartment for so many people to live in," Judy commented, leaning over the table to keep the crumbs from the floor.

"That's why we're going to move," Cathy assured her.

"Now I'll tell you about our new house—well, our new *old* house. We're going to fix it all up."

The door opened and Chris came in. Cathy looked at her seven-year-old sister with extreme disfavor.

Chris's straight, soft blond locks were in the usual disarray; her cheeks glowed wild-rose pink from the cold air. "Chris," Cathy said, "will you please stay out? This is private."

"I want to get my doll," Chris said plaintively. She dragged the doll, in its nightgown, from the lower bed.

"Well, please take her in the other room," Cathy begged.

"I have to put on her dress." Chris squatted to pull a doll's trunk from under the bed and went through it deliberately. Then she sat down on the floor and proceeded to remove the doll's nightgown.

Cathy gave a loud sigh. "Can't you do that in the other room?"

Chris shook her fair head. "Anyhow, this is my room, too," she said.

Cathy and Judy exchanged glances; then Cathy scrambled out of her chair and flung open the door with determination. "Mother!" She marched into the living room. "*Please* can't Chris go somewhere else? Judy and I want to talk."

Mother set her iron down. "I think she'll come out here with me. Chris!" No answer from the bedroom. "Chris, come out here with me a minute, dear," Mother called again.

"I don't want to," Chris said.

"But I would like you to help me with something."

Cathy went back to the bedroom. She knew Chris's stubborn streak, so she tried a different tack. "I think Mother is going to let you iron Jeffy's jerseys," she said

5

in a confidential tone. "But of course if you don't want to I'll do them later. I *love* to iron jerseys!"

Slowly Chris got to her feet, doll in arms, and reluctantly moved toward the bedroom door. Her small face looked unhappy; she wanted to stay. But Cathy hardened her heart. When Chris was out, she closed the door. "There!"

The door swung open again. Jeffy appeared, crawling on the floor and pushing a truck. "Er-er-er-er-er," Jeffy chugged, ignoring his sister and her friend, his face pink as it bent over the truck.

"Jeffy!" Cathy wailed. "Don't come in here!"

"Er-er-er-er-er," said Jeff.

"Judy," Cathy exclaimed, "come on up on the upper berth! Then he can't bother us."

"Er-er-er-er-er," Jeff continued, his tone loud and firm to indicate that he knew what was going on, all right.

"Go on up the ladder. I'll hand you the cookies." Judy climbed the steps and reached down. Nimbly Cathy followed and landed on the bed with a bounce.

"I'm coming up too," Jeff announced suddenly.

"No, you are not!" Cathy quickly reached down, unhooked the ladder, and drew it up out of his reach. "Mother!" she shouted. "Jeffy's bothering us." Mother came in, took Jeffy by the hand, and shut the door behind them.

"I wish I had a key to that old door," Cathy said.

"You could put up a sign," Judy suggested.

"Jeffy can't read. And Chris always pretends she can't when she doesn't want to. Anyhow"—Cathy's tone changed—"it's really their room, too. Now I'll show you my dress-up dress." She dragged the pillow toward her, plunging her arm far into the pillow slip.

6

"Is that where you keep it?" Judy asked in surprise.

Cathy nodded. "It's my secret place, so the children won't find it." She brought out a flowered silk dress and held it up. "Isn't it beautiful?"

"Yes!" Judy's eyes were admiring.

"And I have some jewels to go with it." Cathy's brown hair, curling at the ends, swung forward as she scrambled down to the foot of the bed. "Anybody coming?" she whispered. She reached under the mattress and drew out a somewhat flattened lady's pocketbook. "Oh, that's not the jewels." She gave a giggle. A pair of white gloves appeared next, then a battered compact minus powder. Finally, poking still deeper, Cathy emerged, flushed and clutching a pair of rhinestone earrings with some stones missing, a glittering brooch in the same condition, and a three-strand pearl bracelet dripping a few pearls.

"I'll show you my silver slippers, too!" she exclaimed. Once more she plunged her hand under the mattress, and brought forth the slippers, most of their silver worn off. "Let's dress up!" she cried.

Judy eyed the finery reluctantly. "I better not. I didn't tell my mother I was coming here, so I'd better go home."

"I didn't tell you about the house," Cathy cried. "I didn't tell you about my private suite."

"Private suite!" Judy echoed.

Cathy beamed at her. "I am going to have my very own bedroom and a private bath!" she announced. "And my closet and my bureau are going to be just for me, not for Chris. And nobody can come in my room unless I want them to! And another room, on the other side of my private bath, is going to be the guest

7

room. So if you come and visit me you can sleep in the guest room!"

Judy thought that over, obviously impressed. "Is the house very far away?" she inquired.

"Quite far. It's in Middle Bridge—that's a tiny little town. My mother and daddy have been wanting to move to the country for a long time. The house is very old. It has lots of rooms. And we have a fireplace!"

"You must be rich," Judy said admiringly.

"No." Cathy shook her head. "Only Daddy is going to get a Promotion. He is going to be vice-president of the company. That's why we can buy a house. And I'm going to have a garden with all kinds of beautiful flowers in it. And a bicycle, because it's safe in the country. And maybe we'll get a piano soon and I can take music lessons. I'm crazy to take music lessons!" Cathy was breathless with enthusiasm for these future delights.

Chris opened the door. "What do you want?" Cathy demanded. "Something out of the closet," said Chris. She stood gazing into the closet and Cathy whispered to Judy, "She doesn't really want anything. She just wants to come in."

"I've really got to go, anyhow," Judy said, and Cathy hung the ladder in place. "See you tomorrow," she said, as she got Judy's coat from the living-room closet and opened the door for her.

Cathy picked up her copy of *Heidi* from the living-room table, wandered back to her room, still thinking about the house, and climbed up on her bunk again. She did not bother to shut the door this time. Chris came back and pulled open a bureau drawer. Cathy, reading, was hardly aware of her until Chris said, "What's this, Cathy?"

"Chris!" Cathy scrambled to her knees. "That's my box!" she wailed. "Mother, she's looking in my drawer!"

"I just wanted to see what it was," Chris said calmly, and put the box back.

Cathy spoke severely from her perch. "I will certainly be glad when we move!" The box held only a few pretty shells she had gathered at the seashore. She wouldn't mind giving Chris some if she wanted them, but she pretended they were precious jewels and she did not want her pawing through them.

"When are we going to move?" Chris asked. "And when is Daddy going to get the Promotion?"

Jeffy's head appeared around the door. He was still pushing his truck. "Er-er-er-er-er," said Jeff, crawling into the bedroom.

"Cathy," Chris said wistfully, forgetting her questions, "please come outdoors and play buried trejur with Jeffy and me."

"Not trejur—*treasure!*" Cathy corrected crisply. "You're always getting words wrong. I don't want to play now. I want to read. And when we get in the new house you are not coming into my room—which is going to be the one next to the private bath!"

"So is mine going to be the one next to the private bath—on the other side of it," said Chris.

"No, Chris. You're going to have that room across the hall."

"No!" Chris cried. "That one hasn't got a private bath."

"That doesn't matter, Chris," Cathy said quickly. "You'll be next to Jeffy's room, and think how much fun that will be. You can talk to each other after you're in bed, and if he has a bad dream you can go and get in bed with him."

"But I want a private bath."

"You can just step across—" Cathy had been about to say, "Across the hall to my bathroom," when she had a better idea. "You can just step across Jeffy's room and there is the bathroom. You don't even have to go out in the hall!"

"Well . . ." Chris looked uncertain, and Cathy pressed her advantage. "You see, Chrissy," she explained, "we need that room on the other side of my private bath for a guest room. You might have a guest some time yourself, Chrissy."

Chris looked doubtful, but, having gained her point, Cathy flopped back on her stomach and returned to her book. She paused for a moment to pull off her

10

shoes and socks, wriggling her bare toes luxuriously. Chris went out in the living room to play with Jeff.

But Cathy could not get her mind off the house. She had seen it only twice—gracious and white, set back from the road among its big trees; but it seemed to her she had known it always. Now, lying there on her bunk with her eyes on the page, she saw instead the broad lawns, the drive circling in front of the wide steps.

She saw the long hall with the double living room on the right. The part behind the folding doors would be the TV room, Daddy said. At the left of the hall was another living room, with a side porch. They were going to call that room the library. The dining room was behind it, then the sunny, old-fashioned kitchen, with a tiny bathroom adjoining it.

Upstairs there were three rooms and a bathroom on one side of the hall, two with bath between on the other. It was logical that one of those two should be her own room, because Mother and Daddy wanted the great big room next to the bathroom across the hall, and the tiny room next to that bathroom should be Jeff's. The only remaining question was the one she and Chris had debated: whether Chris should have the other room adjoining Cathy's bath or the room opening into Jeff's. Really it was not Cathy's bathroom; it had a door into the hall and one into the other room. Mother had said, "You children will use that bath." But Cathy thought of it as hers and she was determined to keep Chris out of the room on the other side of it. If Chris had that bedroom she would be in Cathy's room half the time.

Stretched out on her upper bunk for privacy, Cathy tried to imagine what it would be like to have a place where the rest of the family would not be traipsing in and out—where she could close the door and shut out the world. A place where she could leave her precious dress-up clothes and other treasures without having to hide them from the children's inquiring fingers.

She dropped her cheek on her book, gazing dreamily out of the window. She could picture herself dressing for dinner in her own room with the door closed: buttoning on a starched dress, brushing her hair, washing her face, closing her door quietly behind her, and going down the carpeted stairs. Dignified. Grown-up. All the clatter and messiness of the younger children confined in their own two rooms, while her room behind its closed door lay remote, untouchable.

Cathy gave a little sigh and sat up. This lovely dream and the few moments of peaceful retreat had made her feel smoothed out—not so stirred up and cross. After all, she thought, the children come in here all the time because they have no other place. I'll go play with Chris now and be nice to her.

She slid off the top bunk, scorning the ladder. "Chris! Come on and play!"

"They've gone out to the playground," Mother told her, putting the ironing board away.

Cathy went back for her shoes and socks. "I'm going too. For just a little while before I dress for dinner."

Mother smiled at her. Mother understood that Cathy liked the grown-up idea of getting cleaned up for dinner, just as she understood how Cathy longed for her own room. Chris, now, was apt to come to the table with a dirty face and wail her indignation when she was sent to wash.

A few mothers were wheeling their babies along the red-brick walk. Cathy ran toward the fenced-in play space and saw Chris and Jeff swinging. "I'll seesaw with you, Chris!" she shouted.

But as she climbed onto the seesaw she happened to glance toward the walk and saw her father coming briskly up it, carrying his evening paper. He was home early. Perhaps, Cathy thought, he had news about the house.

"There's Daddy. Let's go meet him." She held the seesaw in place for Chris to slip off, then climbed off herself. Jeff was already heading for his father at top speed.

Laughing and breathless, they caught him at the step and clung, while Jeff climbed up like a little monkey. Chris swung on her father's arm. "Hi, Daddy!" Cathy cried. "Is there any more news about the house?"

Daddy, holding Jeff and with Chris still clinging, stooped to kiss his older daughter. "Yes, there's news," said Daddy. "Moving day—February first!"

13

Chapter 2

Moving Day

CATHY AWOKE to the instant knowledge that this was the day they were moving into the new house. Chris was already up, she discovered by leaning over the side of the bed. The bedroom door stood open and voices came from the kitchen.

Cathy threw off the covers and reached for the ladder with her foot. This is the last time I'll sleep in this upper bunk, she thought. I'll sleep in this same bed, but it won't be on top of Chris. I'll be in my own, own room this very night! She could still hardly believe that this wonderful thing was happening.

A suitcase half full of her underclothes and Chris's lay open on the floor. The rug had been rolled up. The curtains were down. Cathy's feet curled from the cold floor as she reached for her bathrobe and scurried into the hall.

Mother was serving oatmeal to Daddy, Chris, and Jeffy in the kitchen. "Hello, dear, pull up a chair. The movers will be here any minute," she said. The shelves were bare of dishes now. Pots and pans peeked from one carton on the floor, canisters of sugar and coffee, jars of peanut butter and jelly, and boxes of beans and rice from another.

Jeffy was saying, "I want to go with you, Daddy."

14

"No, son, there won't be room," Daddy told him. "I have to ride on the van to show them where to go. You'll go in the car with Mother and the girls." Jeff kicked the table rebelliously and dropped his cereal spoon in the dish. Nobody paid any attention, so he picked it up again and went on eating.

The doorbell sounded. Instantly Jeffy dropped his spoon again with a clatter and shot out of his chair and into the other room. Cathy started to follow him. "Finish your breakfast first," Mother told her.

"But I want to get dressed!" Cathy spoke in an urgent whisper. "I don't want those men to see me in this messy old bathrobe!"

Chris said, "I'm through." She slid out of her chair and trotted into the other room. Cathy swallowed her cereal and gulped some milk. She shook her head at Mother's offer of toast and finally escaped to the bedroom. Chris was getting into a pair of dungarees.

"Chris!" Cathy said. "Why are you putting on those old, filthy dungarees?"

"Because we are moving. And I *love* dungarees."

Cathy threw open the closet door and took down a freshly ironed plaid cotton. "Well, I am going to dress up and wear my gold locket," she said. "This a very big, important day, in case you do not realize it."

"Just the same I'm going to wear dungarees." Chris left the room without more ado—also without combing her hair. Cathy shook her head over her departing sister as she got out clean underclothes and robed herself in suitable fashion for this great occasion. She combed her hair, parting it carefully and pinning it trimly into place with a red barrette. Then, surrounded by a strong aura of Summer Garden toilet water, she emerged into the midst of the movers.

The children had gone outdoors to watch the loading. Cathy preferred to stay in the house and see the wide wall spaces open up as the furniture was carried out. She thought she might be helpful to the movers and kept darting forward to drag a chair out of the way or seize a cushion from the sofa until one of the two men said, "Move out of the way, sister. That's a good girl."

"Come help me fold the bedclothes, Cathy," Mother said, coming hurriedly out of the kitchen. Together they stripped the beds, folding sheets and blankets. "You may carry these out to the car," Mother said, handing her a pile. "Tell Chris to come and get some things too." She glanced at Cathy. "Why are you all dressed up?"

"I just wanted to be." Cathy carried the bedding out, but stayed apart from the other children. She wanted the movers to realize that she was much, much older—one of the grown-up members of the family.

The living room was empty now, and Cathy followed the two men as they tramped into the bedroom. As one of them tugged the mattress from the upper bunk, her dress-up treasures lay revealed. "Oh," she cried, "will you please give me that dress and the silver slippers and those jewels and things? I forgot to pack them last night." The man handed them to her and Cathy beamed at him, holding up the dress for him to admire. "These are my most valuable possessions," she explained.

"Yeah?" The man grinned at her. Cathy happily bundled her treasures into the suitcase with her underclothes. For a moment she considered slipping on the silver shoes to impress the moving man. But just then he said, "Out of the way now, girlie," and although his tone was kind, she backed hastily into a corner.

Cathy wondered how they would get the beds through the narrow door. What she saw gave her a shock. One of the men stooped and with a quick jerk pulled the headboard from the rest of the bed. Then he gave another jerk. Why, a bed was not a bed at all, Cathy thought, with an odd feeling that the men might come apart too. A bed was just two flat pieces and a couple of long boards.

The other bedroom was emptied, then the kitchen. Finally there was nothing more of interest going on in the house, so Cathy put on her good coat and went outdoors.

Daddy was carrying armfuls of boxes, and clothes still on their hangers, to load into the car. "Come on, Cathy," he called. "Get the rest of your clothes. And see what else Mother has to bring out."

Cathy took the remaining clothes from the closet and carried them out. "Chris!" she shouted. "Go get your clothes!" At last bedroom and closet were empty. Chris lugged out her doll trunk. The back seat of the car was stacked so high with clothes and other belongings that they hid the back window.

"Children," Mother called from the door, "come in now. We're almost ready to go."

Cathy ran in. Her heart was beating fast as the actual moment approached. Chris followed her, but Jeff, who had stayed close to the open end of the big van all morning, merely hugged a tree and swung himself back and forth as the men fitted the last of the furniture into place.

Daddy washed his hands. The moving men, perspiring and strong-smelling as they tramped past Cathy, came in to take one more look. "Well," Daddy said to

18

Mother, zipping up his sport jacket, "I'll see you in Middle Bridge. You'll probably pass us on the way if you get started pretty quick."

"We're getting started immediately," Mother told him. "Just as soon as I can collect these three and make sure everything is gone."

When Cathy looked out, the back of the van was closed. Daddy climbed up on the high seat with the two men. The heavy motor sprang into life and slowly the loaded van moved out from the curb, turned, and crawled down the street. When its throb had faded Cathy turned from the window. "They're gone!"

Mother echoed her sigh of relief. "Now just let me look around once more and we'll be on our way. Call Jeffy, will you, Cathy?"

Cathy went to the door, but Jeff was not in sight. "Jeffy!" She waited for him to appear around a corner of the house, but he did not come. "Now we've got to go and find that boy!" she declared in exasperation.

"I bet he went in the moving van," Chris said.

Cathy raised her voice. "Maybe he went in the moving van," she called to Mother, who was in the kitchen.

"Oh, no," Mother called back. "Daddy wouldn't take him without telling us."

"I mean inside the moving van," Chris explained.

That brought Mother to the living room. She looked at Chris thoughtfully for a moment, weighing this possibility. Then she spoke quickly. "Both of you run out," she said. "Go to the playground and all around, and call him. And hurry right back!" Then Mother slipped on her own coat and went out too. They scoured Greenacres in a matter of moments. Jeff was not there.

"Come on," Mother said briefly, as they reached the apartment again. "We're overtaking that van! Cathy,

19

carry this box of things from the refrigerator. Take this basket, Chris."

Cathy had intended to visit each room in the apartment for a last time and say good-by. "Good-by, little apartment, I hope some nice people will come to live in you. It was not your fault that you were not big enough." Or something like that. But there was no time. Mother shooed them out, banged the door behind them, and practically ran with them down the walk to the car.

Cathy sat on the edge of the front seat as Mother, a little frown of concentration on her brow, started the engine and headed the car in the direction the van had taken. By this time the van had been gone fifteen minutes.

"Do you think we'll catch it?" Chris inquired.

"I certainly hope so. Chris, did Jeff say anything about going in the van?"

"He just said . . . When the men went into the house, he said, 'We could climb in there and they'd never know.' "

"What did you say?"

"I said, 'No, Jeffy, you might get smothered or something.' "

Cathy grabbed for the window handle as Mother suddenly stepped on the gas and the car gave a plunge. She glanced quickly at her mother, who was looking rather frightened. Cathy was not frightened. This was exciting, just like something in a story, but she felt sorry for her mother. "You should have made him come away or told Daddy!" she said to Chris severely.

"I didn't know he would really do it, Cathy!"

They were on the highway now, and Mother's foot firmly pressed the accelerator until they were passing all the cars on the road. Chris, in the middle, sat up straight trying to see; and Cathy, perched on the edge of her seat, strained for a glimpse of the moving van. Mother finally glanced sidewise at them. "Please sit back," she said. "You make me more nervous, and goodness knows I am nervous enough already!"

"Will Jeffy get smothered?" Chris inquired with interest.

"Chris!" Cathy exploded, with another outraged glance at her mother.

"Oh, I daresay he'll have a lovely trip!" Mother retorted. "No doubt he is pleased as Punch with himself this minute!"

"There's the moving van!" Cathy shrieked. Sure enough, the rear of the van loomed in the distance ahead of them. Just then one of the few traffic lights on the highway flashed red between them and the truck.

"O-o-oh!" Cathy exclaimed, bouncing with impatience. Chris jerked to attention. "I'll make it change! Hocus-pocus!" she cried. The light stayed red. "Hocus-pocus!" Cathy could not resist chiming in on the third try. "*Ho-cus-po-cus!*" they shouted together. The light turned yellow, then green. Cathy and Chris laughed delightedly. "That always makes the light change," Chris said with satisfaction.

Now they really raced to overtake the van, which was out of sight again. Both girls sat erect, eyes straining. This time they saw the rear of the van at the same moment and leaned forward as if to urge the car ahead.

At last they drew alongside the van, Mother sounding the horn long and insistently. As they flew by, Cathy lowered her window and shouted, "Stop! Stop!"

She caught a glimpse of the men's faces turned wonderingly in her direction. Then Mother, who had drawn ahead some distance, stopped at the edge of the highway. The van lumbered along, slowed, and came to a halt behind them.

"Stay in the car," Mother ordered, opening her door.

"No, no!" Cathy couldn't stay there! She had to see. "Oh, please, please let us come too!"

"Well, get out that side then."

By this time Daddy was walking toward them. "Daddy! We think Jeffy is in the moving van!" Cathy cried, running to meet him.

"You think what?" he stared at them unbelievingly.

"Phil, is Jeff in that van?" Mother said quickly. "Chris thinks he is, and we couldn't find him."

"Good heavens!"

It took the moving men only a minute to open the rear of the van. There was no sign of Jeff—only a mattress that practically filled the opening. The men lifted the mattress down.

"Jeff!" Mother called. No answer.

Cathy's legs began to shake. She was frightened now in spite of herself. "Jeff!" she echoed. No answer.

"Hope we don't have to unload the van," one of the men said.

"Jeffy," Chris said, in her soft little voice. "Come on out, Jeffy. You won't get scolded."

There was another moment's silence. "I can't get out," a small voice said.

Instantly the men went into action. They pulled out one of the big upholstered living-room chairs. Behind the chair and under a small table, sat Jeff, rubbing his eyes. It was clear that he had been asleep. He blinked sleepily at the assembled group. Then Jeffy saw his

mother and without a word of explanation he cata-
pulted out of the truck and into her arms, clutching
her around the neck.

The men looked on for a moment, shook their heads,
muttered, and proceeded to reload the chair and the
mattress. Daddy said, "What next?" Chris hugged Jeff
around the legs. Cathy let out a deep breath of happiness and relief. Mother and Jeffy held on to each other.

"O.K.," Daddy said finally. "Now are you ready to go
in the car with Mother?" Jeff nodded and transferred
himself to his father's arms. Daddy carried him to the
car, the others trailing behind.

"I'll get in the back seat," Chris volunteered.

"All right, Chris," Cathy approved. "You're smaller
than I am and it's pretty full back there." She wanted

to get Jeff next to her on the front seat and snuggle him up tight.

With Jeff ensconced between his mother and big sister and Chris riding high on a pile of blankets, Mother gave a brief toot-toot of departure to the van, pulled into the road, and once again they headed for the new house.

CHAPTER 3

In the Snow

CATHY CAME deliberately down the staircase, her hand sliding on the dark, curving rail. She was pretending to be a lady coming down to have the maid serve tea. She turned left through the arch at the foot of the stairs, swept into the living room, and seated herself with elegance in a Windsor chair.

She was wearing the high-heeled silver slippers and the flowered dress fastened with the brooch. She had tied the gown at the waist with a black velvet ribbon. On her head perched a flowered hat. She wore the white gloves and carried the handbag.

Waiting politely for her tea, Cathy glanced through the window. Snow was still drifting down, though the storm that had swept the valley since the night before had almost blown itself out. What a good thing they had got here before the blizzard! Cathy gave a little shiver in the comfortable room and looked at the fireplace. If only she could have a fire in it! Daddy and Mother had been too busy getting unpacked to build one.

There was not too much furniture in the big high-ceilinged living room; still, it looked nice, Cathy thought. They could buy lots more things when Daddy got the Promotion. She got up and wandered into the

smaller room behind the folded-back doors. This was the TV room. Behind that was a small room that the previous occupants of the house had used for a laundry. Cathy paused to look out of the laundry window. The yard stretched back to an old gray barn, and beyond the barn lay the remnant of a small orchard. There were fruit trees there—apple, cherry, and peach, but Daddy said there probably would not be much fruit. Beyond the orchard and the far-reaching fields the low hills were obscured by a veil of snow.

Cathy walked from the TV room into the hall and wandered across to the dining room. A clatter came from the kitchen as Mother stowed dishes and pans in the cupboards. The other children were out in the snow, and Daddy was off somewhere. How strange it felt with no one around!

Abandoning her tea party, Cathy went back upstairs and walked slowly into one bedroom and then another, her high heels clicking on the bare floors. It was a good feeling to have so many rooms to go into —so many rooms, all so empty and silent. Something inside her gave a great stir, like a cat waking from sleep, and stretched luxuriously.

She went into her own room and sat down on the bed to look around and mentally decorate it. Nothing had been done here for a long time. The walls were faded and soiled. The room held only her bed and the bureau and one of the chairs from their old bedroom.

I would like yellow paint, Cathy thought dreamily, gazing around, so it will always look as if the sun were shining. And I would like that shiny material with little rosebuds in it for draperies and my bedspread, with white ruffles under it. And I'll have a dressing table. Mother had said they would manage a dressing table, perhaps even before the Promotion.

She went through the bathroom, which also needed paint. The adjoining bedroom was even worse than her own. Still, it would be a nice room when it was painted and they had bought some furniture. She could picture Judy coming to visit and herself saying good night, in a grown-up way, and closing the doors between the rooms. On second thought, though, it would be more fun just to close the doors into the hall and scamper back and forth between their rooms, giggling as much as they felt like.

Cathy could hardly wait until these rooms were all decorated and furnished! She went down to the kitchen to talk to Mother.

"My goodness," Mother said, reaching to set the waffle iron on a shelf. "You haven't even hung up your clothes. Let's have a little order here before we start painting."

"But I can't *wait* till my room is fixed up!" Cathy climbed the stairs again, this time not nearly as much an elegant lady as an impatient little girl. Her dresses still lay on the chair where she had dumped them the day before. Cathy sighed and looked at the still unpacked suitcase.

Her treasures were there: the rest of the "jewels," the empty compact, an almost empty lipstick, old ribbons and flowers. Now that she had a bureau to herself she could use a whole drawer for dress-up things instead of hiding them under the mattress. What unbelievable luxury! Cathy lovingly unpacked her belongings and laid them neatly in the drawer. There!

I'm going up to the attic, she decided. With the children outdoors and Mother way off downstairs, the whole house was her own, and she still felt that strong urge to reach out into every corner and enjoy possession to the full.

She had been in the attic yesterday and, noticing a pile of old books, she had made a mental note that she would go through them. She went up the steep stairs on tiptoe, the silence of the house hushing her steps.

Cathy looked around the dim, raftered space stretching back to darkness under the sloping roof. She could see a couple of old trunks and other objects back there. This is the tower of a castle, she thought. And I am a princess who lives in the castle. Still in her trailing finery and flowered hat, the princess went over the dusty pile of books and instantly forgot everything else. The first book on the stack was a green-covered volume entitled *Five Little Peppers*. Cathy read the first page, carried the book to the top step near the windows, and sat down.

She had not heard the bell ring, but some time later she raised her head, conscious of voices far below. She listened; then, taking the book with her, she tiptoed down the stairs and hung over the balustrade. "I'll call Cathy. She's upstairs somewhere," she heard Mother say. Mother started up the stairs and then saw her. "Oh, there you are, dear. Come on down." She gave a second look. "Put something else on."

Cathy slipped off her trailing gown and selected a pink skirt and blouse. She folded a fresh white handkerchief carefully so its points protruded smartly from her blouse pocket. She brushed her hair and swished on some Summer Garden. She glanced down, saw the silver slippers, and decided to keep them on. They looked so beautiful and made her feel so grown-up. Then she descended the stairs to the living room.

A lady and a girl about her own age were sitting there with Mother. Mother turned toward Cathy with a smile. "Mrs. McArdle, this is my older daughter, Cathy. The McArdles are our next-door neighbors, dear. And this is Martha. She is nine years old too."

Cathy gave her hand to Mrs. McArdle and said, "How do you do?" Then she said, "Hello," and sat down near Martha, glancing at her quickly. Martha had red hair and a sweet little freckled face. For a few minutes the two girls sat shyly listening to their mothers.

"We were out late last night," Mrs. McArdle said. "When I saw you were here this morning, I decided to come right over and get acquainted."

"They brought us the most delicious-looking dish of macaroni and cheese you ever saw," Mother told Cathy. "And we are so glad to know our neighbors."

Cathy caught Martha's glance at the silver shoes. She wiggled her feet. "I was all dressed up when you came," she explained with a chuckle, while her mother and Mrs. McArdle talked. "I had on a beautiful dress and a flowered hat. Do you like to dress up?"

Martha nodded. "I love to."

"Would you like to see our house?" Cathy inquired.

"All right." Martha looked pleased. "I've been here before, when the Cartrights lived here. But I'd like to see it again," she added politely.

"Of course, practically everthing has to be done to the place," Mother was explaining to Mrs. McArdle, as the girls departed.

Cathy took Martha over the first floor. On the way upstairs she apologized. "It looks awful up here. But it's going to look just beautiful when we get everything done. This is my room," she said as they went into it. "It is going to be painted yellow. And I am

30

going to have a flowered bedspread and curtains and everything just beautiful. This is my private bath." She led the way through. "And this room is also part of my private suite. Only it's going to be a guest room."

Martha seemed impressed. They made a tour of the attic and on the way down she said, "What grade are you in?"

"Fourth."

"Then you'll be in my class. There are only ten in the class," Martha told her. "You'll be the eleventh."

"I saw the school—the outside," Cathy said.

"It's a nice school. We only have four rooms. The kindergarten and the fifth and sixth grades go to the consolidated school."

Cathy nodded. "I know. My little brother is going there. He is delighted, because he is going on the school bus."

They were back in Cathy's room now, and Martha glanced toward the window. "Look," she exclaimed. "It's stopped snowing!" Cathy looked out and saw a pale streak of sunlight lying across the cold, snowy landscape. "Let's go out!" Martha cried. "Have you got a sled?" Cathy shook her head. "You can use my brother's," Martha said. "Come on. Let's go see if Gretchen can come out."

Cathy started down, then remembered the slippers. "I better take these off," she said laughing. "They would be silly in the snow, wouldn't they!"

The air felt damp but deliciously fresh and cold, as the two girls waded through the snow to Martha's house. They found the sleds in the garage and pulled them along, heading across the road.

"We cut between these houses," Martha said, "over to South Street. Gretchen lives next to the post office.

We only have two streets, North and South," she explained. Then she pointed down the road to a span crossing a narrow stream. Beyond the bridge the road curved into the woods. "See that bridge? That's the end of the town. The two streets come together there."

A brown cocker came through the snow, wet and panting, and Martha stopped. "Hello, Beans," she said. "Hello, Beans," Cathy echoed, patting his head.

"That's the store over there. Want me to introduce you to Mrs. Himmel? Gretchen!" Martha shouted to a girl pulling a sled. "We'll be over in a minute. Wait!"

She led Cathy into the grocery, which smelled of coffee and pickles, and presented her importantly to a stout, friendly lady behind the counter.

"And there is the post office next door," Martha pointed out, as they went outdoors again.

Gretchen was smaller than Martha and Cathy, with curly dark hair and a friendly smile. "Some of the kids

32

have gone up to Terhune's Hill to coast," she told them. "Do you want to go?"

"Sure!" Martha cried. They headed back toward North Street and turned up the road from Cathy's house. They had gone only a few steps, drawing their sleds, when Cathy heard cries behind her. "Cath-y! Wait!"

She explained. "That's my sister and brother. I'll have to wait for them."

Chris and Jeff were plodding toward them, covered with snow, happy and out of breath. "Come on if you want to," Cathy told them. "We're going coasting. Only you haven't got any sleds."

"We don't care!" The frosty air billowed from Chris's mouth and her cheeks were scarlet.

A snowplow was already on the job and passed them as they trooped along. Jeff dropped behind to watch it with fascinated interest. Ahead on their left Cathy saw a deep, gently sloping field. At the top a group of children shouted and ran with their sleds, dropping to the ground with a force that carried them well down the slope.

"The snow is packed down some already," Martha said. "Come on. Let's go up."

In the deep snow the hill seemed steep to climb. When they reached the top, Martha and Gretchen were on their sleds and coasting in a moment. Cathy felt uncertain. She had never done any real coasting. They had seldom had enough snow in the city, and the streets were too full of traffic. She watched the way the others ran and flopped on their sleds, but she didn't think she could do that.

"Come on, Cathy!" Martha cried, puffing uphill.

"I don't know how."

"Lie down on the sled—on your stomach," Martha instructed her. "I'll give you a push."

Cathy stretched out awkwardly and Martha ran behind, giving a good strong push. The sled went down, but not as fast as the others.

"Let me do it! Let me, Cathy!" Chris cried, when she climbed back.

"Do you want to use my sled for a while?" Gretchen asked Cathy kindly.

"Thank you." Cathy watched a boy as he ran with his sled. "I'm going to try that," she declared. The first time, she hit the sled with a jar that took the wind out of her, but she got a beautiful start. Down the hill she flew, the cold wind stinging her eyes and making her nose prickle. "Oh, I want to do that again!" she cried, laughing aloud as she climbed back up the hill.

But she let Jeff take the sled next. As she stood watching him push off with his feet, Gretchen said, "Does just your family live in that house?"

Cathy nodded. "Yes."

"You must be rich," Gretchen said.

"Oh, no," Cathy said modestly. "But my father is going to get a Promotion. You can come over as soon as I get my bedroom decorated—and my bath," she invited graciously. Gretchen looked at her with respect.

The red sun was setting when Cathy and the others finally headed for home. Their soaked hands and feet were stinging with the cold, but inwardly they were glowing. In front of Martha's house, Cathy handed back her sled. "Thank you, Martha," she said. She felt as if they were old friends now. "I'll see you tomorrow at school."

"I'll watch for you to come by," Martha assured her.

The younger children still had not had their fill of the snow and decided to stay out. Daddy was at home when Cathy went in. "Oh," she gasped, tugging her coat off, "we had the most *fun*! Daddy, won't you please build a fire in the fireplace? My feet are just frozen!"

"Bring in a couple of those small logs from the back porch," Daddy said. "I'll get some kindling."

She helped lug in the logs and watched as her father laid crumpled paper and kindling. The fire ran through the pile, caught, and whipped quickly upward in a clear yellow tongue of flame.

"How lovely and warm!" Cathy sat down on the leather stool in front of the fire and pulled off her socks. She held her icy, red toes in her hands, then stretched them out to the delicious warmth. Soon she remembered something and went upstairs in her bare feet to get it.

When she came back with *Five Little Peppers*, the fire was crackling and snapping in a brisk blaze, the wood smell pungent in the warm room. Reflected flames leaped on the darkening walls. Outside, the red glow in the sky had faded as a cold winter dusk closed in. Cathy pulled a big chair close to the light of the fire and settled herself, bare feet on the stool close to the warmth. With a sigh of perfect contentment, she opened her book.

Chapter 4

A Job of Painting

CATHY, CHRIS, and Mother watched Jeffy set off for kindergarten on the school bus next morning. He climbed on in front of the house, and Cathy saw him slide into a seat and wave with a broad smile.

"He's happy," Chris said placidly.

"It's a good thing," Mother added, as they turned back up the drive, "that it isn't you girls who take the bus, while Jeffy goes to school here. His heart would be broken."

Daddy had taken an early bus to the Springdale station to go to work. It was time for Cathy and Chris to start for school now. Mother was walking over with them to see the teacher, and the three started along the road. Everywhere Cathy looked this morning the snow crust sparkled like millions of diamonds. The glare on the bright white snow struck her eyeballs like a blow.

In front of the McArdle house Martha came to meet them. "Hi, Martha!" Cathy cried.

"Hi." Martha looked happy as she joined them. "You could've cut through the back yards. This is the long way."

"We have to learn these things," Mother told her, smiling.

36

Chris trudged along behind the others. Now she caught up, carrying an armful of snow. "Why are you carrying that? Isn't there enough snow without taking some with you?" Mother inquired, smiling down at her.

"I just like to." Chris's face was rosy with cold, and she took a bite out of the snow she was carrying. "Tastes good!"

They were early, but a few boys and girls were already making snowballs or playing with their sleds outside the red-brick school. Gretchen and another girl worked at building a snow man. When Mother and the two teachers had completed the formalities, Cathy and Chris went out again to play. Chris wandered off with an unoccupied sled. Martha was helping to build the snow man and Cathy joined her, trying to scoop up the snow, so soft and powdery under the thin crust.

She glanced up as a station wagon stopped in front

of the school, delivering a pupil. "There's Bernice," Martha said. She called, "Bernice! Come here! We have a new friend." The girl who came toward them was short and rather pudgy. "This is Cathy. She just moved here," Martha said.

"Hello." Cathy looked at Bernice, and Bernice stared back. Just then someone called and Martha turned away. "Where do you live?" Bernice asked.

"On North Street," Cathy said.

"Which house?"

"Well, it's the house some people named Cartright used to live in."

Bernice looked more interested. "That great big house?" Cathy nodded. Bernice's eyes studied her boldly. "That's a beautiful house," she said.

Cathy was flattered. "It has to have a lot of things done to it," she admitted. "Our bedrooms have to be decorated and we are going to get a lot of furniture. A piano, too, so I can take lessons. When my father gets his Promotion, that is," she added with a modest laugh. Bernice had seemed so impressed that Cathy could not resist boasting a little.

"My father is a farm manager," Bernice said. "We have a new house. It's a ranch house."

"Well, my father is the New York manager of Davis and Company," Cathy replied. "Only he is going to be a vice-president when he gets the Promotion." It had not occurred to her to mention any of this to Martha, but for some reason she felt called on to explain to Bernice what an important man Daddy was.

"Do you want to come over to my house some day after school?" Bernice asked.

Cathy felt flattered. "I'll ask my mother."

Cathy liked Mrs. Franz, the teacher. Mrs. Franz was

not young. Her black hair was touched with iron gray and she had kind brown eyes and dark skin, deeply lined. The school was old, but the shabby room was large and sunny. Green plants lined the broad sills; bright drawings circled the room above the chalkboards. Chris's room was downstairs. Cathy accepted the reader and arithmetic book Mrs. Franz gave her and ran through the pages of the reader longingly. She would take it home this afternoon and read the whole book.

At noon she and Martha and Chris hurried home. The air was not so sharp now, and snow dripped from the trees. Over the lunch table Cathy and Chris—and Jeff, glowing from his two-way bus trip—described school for Mother.

"And there's a girl, Bernice—they have a new ranch house—she asked me if I could come over some day after school," Cathy reported. "May I?"

Mother sipped her soup and passed the crackers to Jeff. "If you'd like to, dear," she said, "so long as I know where she lives. If I were you, though, I would take my time about making friends. Sometimes it is better to wait until you have a chance to know people."

"Good!" Chris said. "I want you to play with me."

"I don't know whether I am going to play with you much," Cathy remarked tartly. "I want to paint my room. Can we get some paint and start this afternoon?" she asked Mother.

"We can't get any paint today," Mother said. "Besides, Daddy will have to do the painting."

"Well, let's order the paint so he can start tonight. I want my room done first."

Chris gave a small, wistful moan. Jeff took the cue instantly and said, "No, mine!"

"Maybe we can do a wall of each," Cathy suggested.

"No, we cannot, thank you," Mother said firmly.

Chris sighed. "Let's get some painters to do it."

"We can't afford to hire painters to paint this whole big house," Mother told her.

"When Daddy gets the Promotion we can," Chris said smugly.

"Do you want to wait for that?" Mother asked.

"*No!*" Cathy and Chris shouted together, with Jeff chiming in.

"Just be patient then, and we'll get all your rooms done."

That afternoon the Middle Bridge Brownie Troop was meeting. Cathy and Chris rushed home at three o'clock, scrambled into Brownie dresses, and picked up some pennies. They had been Brownies in the city, so it was exciting to find a troop waiting for them here.

The meeting was at Gretchen Lacy's house, and Gretchen's mother was the leader. Most of the girls in Cathy's and Chris's classes were in the troop, and the school bus brought a load from the Chestnut Hollow school. Cathy looked around at the bright, friendly faces during the business meeting. It gave her a good comfortable feeling to know she was part of this nice group.

When they went home from the meeting, Cathy led Chris through the short cut between the houses that Martha had showed her. The dog that had greeted Martha came out, wagging his tail, and Cathy patted his head. "Hello, Beans." He seemed to remember her. The comfortable feeling of belonging glowed inside her.

At supper Chris said dreamily, "Gretchen's mother has a funny name—Mrs. Silky."

"Silky!" Cathy cried. "Mrs. *Lacy*, Chris!"

"I mean Lacy." Chris looked embarrassed. Cathy laughed and Jeff joined in.

"Cathy!" Mother said reproachfully.

"Well, she's always getting words wrong!"

"I am not always, Cathy Leonard!" Chris said, but Cathy giggled.

Saturday morning all three children watched in the upper hall as Daddy opened the paint that had been delivered, to show them the colors. The sunny yellow, just the shade she had wanted, was for Cathy's bedroom and bath. The pale pink was for Chris, the green for Jeff.

"Which room do we do first?" Daddy asked.

"Mine!" Cathy shouted.

Chris said nothing; Cathy was aware of her silence. As Daddy began to stir the yellow paint, Chris slipped away into her bedroom. Cathy said nothing, but her conscience was beginning to trouble her. She had talked Chris out of taking the room next to her bath, and now her own room was being painted first. It really wasn't fair, she admitted to herself. Finally she whispered to Daddy, glancing toward Chris's closed door, "You can do hers first, Daddy."

"Well, make up your mind," Daddy said cheerfully, still stirring the paint.

"Yes, hers!"

"O.K."

She went in to tell Chris that Daddy was going to do her room first. Chris was face down on the bed.

"It's all right, Chrissy," Cathy said softly. "Daddy is going to paint your room first." She patted her sister's back.

Chris sat up, tousled, her nose pink and her eyes wet. "All right," she said. "Thank you!" she added impulsively. Cathy felt contrite. Chris was a sweet little girl. She demanded so little and took it for granted that Cathy's rights came first. Cathy was suddenly aware that she often took advantage of Chris's meekness. Yes, she was glad she had told Daddy to paint Chris's room first.

"But could I just start my room while you are doing Chris's?" she begged, as Daddy covered the floor and furniture in Chris's room with old cloths and paper.

"No, we are doing one room at a time."

"Then I'll do some of Chris's!" Cathy was determined to speed up this job so her own room could be done.

"O.K. We'll see how well you can do it." Daddy showed her how to use the paint roller, and she tried it while he used a paintbrush on the woodwork. Painting with a roller was fun. She squeezed the excess paint off carefully and pressed the roller hard against the wall, enjoying the smooth, free roll and the little sucking sound. The wall looked beautifully painted when she took the roller away. Chris and Jeff watched enviously.

That night Mother cleaned Cathy's paint-daubed hands with naphtha. "I hope I can get enough off," she said, "to make you respectable for Sunday school tomorrow."

They were all going to church, for Sunday school in the old gray church across the street was held at the same time as the church service. In the morning, however, Jeffy announced, "I don't want to go."

"Then I can't go," Mother said. "I am not going to leave you here alone."

But Jeffy changed his mind when he saw the girls emerge, pink-cheeked and shining from their baths, and dressed in their rustly blue taffetas. Hastily Mother scrubbed him clean, and the five Leonards went down the drive and across the road together.

Cathy liked this Sunday school, in the big, warm, old-fashioned room with the red carpet. It developed, too, that there was a junior choir to which she and Chris could belong. They could wear dark-red robes and black velvet caps and march into church with the others. Cathy was skipping with happiness when they met Mother and Daddy.

Jeff wanted to be in the junior choir too. "In a couple of years, dear," Mother told him, but he was cross and went off by himself.

Cathy went outdoors to look for him when dinner was ready. Jeff was sitting on top of the chimney of the outdoor fireplace, his feet inside the chimney.

"Jeff," Cathy exclaimed. "You come down!"

"Why?"

She was about to say, Because it is dangerous and you might fall, or, Because it is wet and you will take cold. But she thought better of it. "Because dinner is ready and we are having roast beef. Come on, Jeffy, I'll help you down."

She reached up and grasped him around the waist, but when she tried to drag him off the chimney Jeff gave a yelp: "You're hurting me!" The chimney was so narrow that the only way to get his legs out was to lift him up. Cathy finally ran to call her father.

43

Daddy came striding out, lifted Jeff straight into the air, and set him on the ground. "Stay out of chimneys, young man," he said. "Who do you think you are—Santa Claus?"

Chris's room was finished that night. Mother washed the floor and put down small braided rugs; then they set the bed back in place. A new chest of drawers and a small rocking chair had come. The room still looked bare, but so fresh and dainty that Cathy, who stood in the door, was consumed with envy in spite of herself.

Chris trotted around, putting her doll trunk and doll bed in place and singing to herself, "Pink can come, pink can come, pink can come, pink can come . . ."

"Stop singing that silly thing, Chris!" Cathy cried.

Chris began putting her doll to bed. "I'll sing the second verse. "Blue can go, blue can go, blue can go . . ."

"Cut it *out*, Chris!" Cathy almost stamped her foot. She flounced into her own room, fingers in her ears. In a minute she heard Chris droning absent-mindedly, "Cut it out, cut it out, cut it out, cut it out."

Cathy held her hands over her ears and ran downstairs. It was bad enough to be so envious of Chris's new room that she could hardly stand it, without having to listen to that dopey song over and over and over. She went into the living room where Mother and Daddy were relaxing. "Can't I start my room after school tomorrow, Daddy?" she begged. "Oh, please let me!"

Finally Daddy agreed. "O.K., start in if you want to, if your mother is willing to supervise."

Next day Cathy rushed home. "Where's the paint?"

she demanded breathlessly. "I'm going to put on my dungarees." She went flying upstairs.

Jeff climbed after her. "Cathy," he said, coming into her room, "I want my room painted next."

"Oh, Jeffy, we'll do that right after we finish mine." Cathy was rushing into her work clothes.

"No! I want mine done now." The corners of Jeff's lower lip began to tremble. Suddenly he flung an arm over his eyes and turned toward the door.

Instantly Cathy's heart melted. "Jeffy, we'll paint your room next. Don't cry, Jeffy." She ran after him and put her arms around him. "Cathy will start painting your room right this very minute, so don't cry!" Jeffy wiped his eyes, sniffed up the tears, and trotted trustingly downstairs with her to get the paint.

Cathy sighed deeply as she stood in the middle of Jeffy's room. Once more she was bitterly disappointed. Yet how could she let Jeffy feel bad? Well, she might as well get this room painted as quickly as she could. The room was small and maybe Daddy could finish the first coat tonight.

"Here's the paint," Mother said, "and here is the roller. Do as far up as you can reach." She spread cloths to protect the floor and watched as Cathy got started. "You're doing fine," she said finally. "I'll be up again in a few minutes."

Cathy painted. Jeff sat on the floor and watched. Chris, with her own room finished, had lost interest and was outdoors. Finally Cathy gave a sigh and paused to rest.

"Can I paint?" Jeff said.

"Oh, no, Jeffy, you can't. You're not old enough. I'm just going downstairs to get something to eat," Cathy told him. "Then I'll paint some more." She put

45

the roller down carefully in its pan, wiped her hands on a cloth, and went downstairs for some bread and jelly.

She was just spreading the currant jelly when a bloodcurdling screech from upstairs made her jump and drop a crimson blob on the kitchen table. Mother, paring vegetables, dropped her knife and headed for the hall. Upstairs, Jeff was crying as if his heart would break.

"What's the matter, Jeff?" Mother called, reaching the top of the stairs with Cathy at her heels.

They had no need to ask. The paint can was tipped over, and green paint was rapidly spreading over the floor of Jeffy's room. The roller lay on the floor. Mother gave a startled yelp, righted the paint can, and grabbed a cloth. "Get a lot of newspapers, Cathy!" she cried. "Hurry up!"

Together they mopped up the floor. "I'll scrub it with turpentine," Mother said. It was not until they paused to catch their breaths that Cathy noticed Jeffy, who had stopped crying to watch the proceedings.

"Mother, look at Jeffy!"

Jeffy's hands were covered with paint. His face, where his hands had rubbed at the tears, was streaked with green. There was green paint in his ears, up his nose, on his arms, in his hair, and all over his overalls.

"And I shall scrub you with turpentine, too!" Mother cried.

"No!" Jeff shouted in alarm, heading for the stairs.

"Cathy, we've got to get hold of him," Mother said. "He'll get paint on everything. I'll get the naphtha—that isn't so strong. See if you can catch him."

Cathy went down cautiously. "Jeffy!" she called

softly. There was a sound in the living room, and as she went in she saw Jeff disappear into the TV room. She went back into the hall. Jeff, who had been peeking into the hall from the TV room, promptly ran across into the dining room. Cathy went into the library to head him off, and he scooted back into the hall and hovered there, watching to see which way she would turn.

"He won't come!" Cathy called.

"He cannot go to kindergarten tomorrow unless we get that paint off," Mother said firmly, from the top of the stairs.

The prospect of missing the bus trip was too much. "I have to see something first," Jeff announced, and disappeared into the TV room. Then, having saved his dignity, he trotted upstairs.

They made it as painless as they could. "Jeffy Leonard, who ever heard of green hair!" Cathy cried. Jeff laughed through his tears of protest and finally emerged more pink than green.

"I guess we'll have to paint that floor green, too," Mother decided. "I can stand an all-green room, but I do not care to have an all-green boy, thank you."

Daddy finished giving Jeffy's room the first coat. It seemed to Cathy that as he worked he had a preoccupied air. Was he cross with them, because of the accident with the paint, she wondered.

"Do my room the minute you finish Jeffy's!" she begged.

"No, I can't," he told her rather shortly. "I've got to rest for a while."

"Oh!" Cathy wailed.

"That's enough, Cathy," Daddy said briefly. "Don't nag."

Cathy was silent, but when she went into her room to go to bed its dinginess struck her with special force after the bright cleanness of Chris's room and Jeff's. How could she wait? And when would she ever get the dressing table and the other furnishings she longed for!

She pressed her lips together. Those children, having to have their rooms done before hers was touched! She brushed her teeth quickly, jumped into bed, and covered her head, hiding her hurt. Her room was just never going to be beautiful, the way she had pictured it! And the guest room wouldn't be, either. Tears of frustration welled into Cathy's eyes as she lay there in the dark under the covers.

There was a small sound, and she lowered the blanket. She could see her door opening softly, as the light from the hall shone in. Someone stood there motionless. Then as Cathy stirred, a small, sturdy figure pattered across the floor toward her. "I had a bad dream. I want to get in your bed, Cathy," Jeff said.

"All right, Jeffy, come on." Cathy moved over, and he scrambled quickly under the covers to snuggle against her. She covered him and he moved confidently closer, his solid little back warm against her. He smelled of naphtha. Tears of envy and impatience still in her eyes, Cathy put her arm around her little brother.

CHAPTER 5

Cathy's Room Is Ready

CATHY STOOD, a week later, in her newly painted bedroom and gazed around, joy in her heart.

The sun streamed in brilliantly this morning, but even on a dark day the clear yellow of the walls and the creamy woodwork would give an effect of sunlight. There was still very little furniture—just the bed, bureau, straight chair, and table. Cathy had made her bed, and everything was beautifully neat.

Mother had promised her a dressing table and stool soon. Cathy could hardly wait to sit down like a lady to brush her hair. I think I'll just get out my powder puff and lipstick, she thought, rummaging in the drawer. She found the empty compact and worn-down lipstick and laid them on the bureau. She would not really use them, of course, except perhaps when she played dress-up, if Mother would let her. But it made her feel grown up to have them lying there.

I don't feel like going to school today, Cathy thought, in a fever of impatience to get her room all fixed up. I feel like going to Springdale and buying the things for my room—the dressing table and the flowered material for my bedspread and some frilly white stuff. What else? She looked around. I know what I'd like in here, she thought suddenly. Bookshelves! She had lots of books. How wonderful it would be to bring them all in here and have them to herself! But Cathy felt extremely doubtful about Mother's buying shelves for her right now.

Into Cathy's mind suddenly came a picture of some old boards she remembered seeing in a dark corner of the barn. Just then Chris called upstairs, "Cathy, it's time to go!" Cathy reluctantly picked up her reading book from the table and turned slowly toward the door. "Good-by, dear room," she said softly, throwing a kiss. "I'll be back as soon as I can."

At recess Cathy bubbled with the news about her room. "My room is the yellow room," she related

happily. "Then we have the pink room—that's Chris's —and the green room—my little brother's. My mother and daddy's room is going to be blue. And my private bath is yellow. The guest room is going to be painted a beautiful rose color."

In the little circle of girls on the playground, Martha's blue eyes shone at her friend's pleasure. Gretchen's face, turned to Cathy's, was full of admiration for such elegance. It was when Cathy happened to look from Martha's smile to Bernice that the contrast in expression gave her an unpleasant shock. Bernice looked, somehow, as if she were envious yet gloating, too, because she knew a girl who lived in a huge, fine house full of pink, green, blue and yellow rooms.

"Well, anyhow," Cathy concluded happily, "as soon as I get my dressing table and stuff, you can all come over."

When they got home after school that afternoon, Mother said, "I have to go into Springdale, girls. Do you want to come along?"

"Yes," said Chris.

"Oh, can we get the things for my room?" Cathy cried.

"I can't take the time today, honey."

"Then I don't want to go," Cathy said. She was thinking that this might be a good time to investigate those boards in the barn. "You don't want to go, do you, Jeff?" she said. She might need his help if the boards proved suitable.

"I want to stay with you," Jeff said agreeably.

They went out to the barn after they had each eaten a banana. The barn was dank-smelling and dark and seemed colder than outdoors. Cathy found the boards where she remembered noticing them. She could see, even in this dim light, that they were rough and weather-beaten and very dirty, but they would hold books. "Help me carry these out, Jeff," she said.

Outside in the light the boards looked even worse. Cathy felt a twinge of doubt. But she was not to be stopped by dirt. "Let's carry them to the house, Jeff," she decided, "and I'll give them a good washing."

They lugged the two best boards up to the back door and laid them down. "Now I'll bring out a pail of water and the scrubbing brush," Cathy said briskly. But when she got the pail of soapy water outdoors she suddenly realized how cold it was to do such a job. She had brought cold water and it seemed as if her wet hands would freeze to solid ice. "We'd better take them in the house," she decided.

Cathy carefully laid newspapers on the clean kitchen floor. Then she got down on her knees and scrubbed the upper side of a board vigorously with soapsuds. Grime, dust, and dirty water oozed out.

"My goodness, this is dirty!" Cathy sat back on her heels. "I think I'll put it in the sink to rinse it. First I'll wash the other side." They turned the board over, and she gave the other side a scrubbing. "Now, Jeffy, help me get one end into the sink."

Jeff stood valiantly on tiptoe holding one end high, while Cathy got a pan of clean water and poured it down the board. "This is the way they rinse Mother's hair in the beauty parlor," she told Jeff with a giggle. "Let's play I'm a hairdresser and I'm rinsing a lady's hair." She rinsed and rinsed, and the dirty water ran partly into the sink and partly on the floor. Puffing with the effort, Jeff helped her to reverse the board, and Cathy rinsed the other end. "Now we'll let it dry," she declared with satisfaction.

They were rinsing the second board when Mother and Chris walked in. Mother gave one look at her kitchen. Cathy, following her horrified gaze, saw for the first time that the kitchen floor around the sink was a veritable mud puddle. "I'll clean it up," she said quickly. "We were just washing these boards so I can make bookshelves of them."

"You certainly will clean it up!" Mother assured her. "I washed this floor this morning!"

"And look at those messy newspapers," Chris exclaimed.

"Oh, be still, Chris," Cathy said impatiently. "I *said* I would clean it up!" She changed quickly to a positive note. "These shelves are all clean. As soon as they are dry, I'll take them upstairs. There will be much more room for books down here, Mother, when I get mine out of the way."

"What are you going to use to prop the shelves up?" Mother inquired doubtfully.

"Stones," Cathy said. "Jeff will help me dig some up."

"Oh, no, Cathy," Mother exclaimed. "You can't dig stones out of frozen ground. They'd be so dirty, anyway!"

"Well, I'll find something else then. Come on, Jeff, help me." She started to pick up one of the boards.

"I'll help you if it must go upstairs," Mother said.

They were halfway up with the damp board when Cathy, leading the way, suddenly gave a squeal and stopped.

"Would you mind not knocking me downstairs?" Mother exclaimed. "What's the matter?"

"I've got an idea!" Cathy crowed. "I know what I can prop the shelves up with. Oh, goody!"

"What?" Mother asked suspiciously.

"I don't want to tell. You won't mind—really, Mother dear!"

"We'll see about that, Cathy dear," Mother retorted.

"And I don't want anyone in my room till it's ready!"

Chris and Jeff had followed the board, however, and had no intention of accepting banishment. Both sat down firmly on the top step. "Very well, stay there," Cathy said loftily.

She climbed the stairs to the attic, ignoring Chris's and Jeff's whispers and giggles, gathered an armful of the old books, and descended, eyeing the expectant pair with the expression of a cat that has swallowed a canary. She made two more trips.

"Excuse me, *please*," she said, with exaggerated politeness, squeezing between Chris and Jeff to go downstairs. When she had taken all her own books from the library shelves she headed for the kitchen. "Will you help me take the other shelf up?" she asked her mother breathlessly.

When the shelf had been deposited in her room, she said sternly, "Now nobody can come in!" and closed the door. She worked busily for quite a while before she threw it open. "Now you may come in! Mother, come see my shelves!" she shouted down the stairs.

The gray, weathered shelves stood against the wall beside the bed, each propped by two piles of the less interesting attic books. Each shelf, to be sure, was higher at one end than the other. "The books wouldn't come out even," Cathy explained, "but that doesn't matter." She had set her own books on the shelves along with the best of the attic lot. Her doll, full skirt outspread, triumphantly occupied the middle of the top shelf.

Chris and Jeff were as pleased as Cathy. Mother gave her grimy, disheveled daughter a hug and said, "Honey, it looks just lovely!"

"Now," Cathy said, with a tired but happy sigh, her face streaked with dirt, "if we could just get the other things!"

"We will," Mother assured her.

Mother kept her promise. On Saturday she and Cathy went to Springdale and bought organdy, flowered chintz, and a small dressing table and stool. Chris wanted a patchwork quilt on her bed and did not care about a dressing table. Mother worked late at night at her sewing machine, and in a week's time Cathy's room was transformed.

Cathy had scarcely ever known such complete happiness as she felt at the moment when she stood at last in her finished bedroom. Ruffled curtains, crisp and dainty, crossed at the windows. Organdy skirts matched them below the chintz bedspread and around the dressing table. A small blue rug lay on the dark floor.

"Oh!" Cathy gasped in ecstasy. "Isn't it *beautiful*, Mother!"

It was her own. When Mother went out, Cathy closed the door and sat silently by herself to take in the beauty, the wonder of a dream come true at last.

She pulled her father upstairs that night before he

was out of his coat. Daddy was properly admiring. But even in the midst of her joy Cathy thought, glancing at him, that he did not seem quite as enthusiastic as he ought to be. Almost immediately the thought slipped from her mind.

It was mid-March now. The snow was gone; but deep winds boomed ceaselessly in the tops of the pine trees around the house, and the countryside lay drab and brown. Chris and Jeff were always outdoors. Cathy preferred to stay in her room and read or dress up. When Mother shooed her out into the fresh air, she sometimes crawled into a secret place where the younger children could not find her. This was her pine house—a dark, sheltered cave made by the low-lying branches of the big pine tree near the side porch. At other times she forgot that she wanted to be alone, and raced shouting through the yard with the others.

In school the fourth-grade girls were writing a play about a princess, which they planned to produce with the girls of all four classes in the cast. Cathy yearned secretly to be the princess and wear beautiful flowing gowns; and when Martha suggested her for the role and the others agreed, she was overcome.

"Let's ask Mrs. Franz to give us some costumes from her trunk, Cathy," Gretchen suggested. "She has the most beautiful costumes, that some mothers gave her."

After school Mrs. Franz took the group down into a basement storeroom. Cathy gasped as she drew out a flaming rose chiffon evening dress. "Oh, that would be just right for the princess!" she cried. Mrs. Franz held up a sapphire-blue velvet cape. "That one too!"

Martha exclaimed. "And I can bring my silver slippers!" Cathy cried, clasping her hands. "Hey, kids, we must have a lot of scenes!" The more scenes, she thought, the more glamorous costumes she could wear.

Chris had found her way to the basement. "Can I be in the play?" she inquired plaintively.

"I guess so," Cathy said.

"What can I be?"

"A witch," Cathy informed her carelessly, dipping into the trunk. Chris gave a little moaning sound, which her sister ignored. "Cathy, do I *have* to be a witch?" Chris asked a few minutes later.

"No," Cathy said. "You can be a lady in waiting." Chris was satisfied.

Bernice was to be the king, Martha the queen, Gretchen the prince. "If the play is good," Mrs. Franz promised, "you may give it for the P.T.A."

"How can we give the play when we don't have any flatform?" Chris asked.

"Not *flatform*, Chris—platform! And anyhow, you mean *stage!*" Cathy laughed aloud and the other girls echoed her. Chris's cheeks flushed pink.

They practiced at recess and after school. "Oh, dear," Cathy the princess cried, "my father the king will not let me marry the prince!"

The king emerged, arms folded nobly across his chest. "I told you to stay in your room!" thundered the king. "O.K.," said the princess, obediently hustling off. Mrs. Franz said that was enough for today.

Cathy floated home from rehearsal on rosy clouds. "Oh, I just love my darling school! And my darling house and my darling room, too!" she shouted in Mother's direction, as she headed for the stairs.

She always went to her room after school. And

for some reason which she hardly understood, Cathy always tiptoed between the top of the stairs and her door. It was almost as if she were afraid it would go away if it heard her coming. She held her breath, too, as she softly opened the door to her room. There it was, as fresh and pretty and peaceful as she had left it. She stood for a second looking in, loving it. Then she heard Chris coming up and quickly closed the door behind her. She had decided to dress up and go on being a princess. "Keep out," she told Chris through the door.

"Why?"

"Just because." Cathy got out the flowered dress and slipped it on. But maybe I will let Chris play, she decided, relenting as she buckled the silver shoes. She can carry my train. And Jeff can be a page. She opened the door and shouted, "Jeff!"

"What is it?"

"Get a pillow," Cathy instructed him. "I'll make a golden crown and you can be the princess's page." They were still playing the entrancing game when Daddy came home and Mother called Cathy to set the table.

At dinner that night it seemed to Cathy again that Daddy was quiet and absent-minded. She had noticed lately that he seemed strange. She glanced at him once or twice to try and figure out what was wrong.

It was after the dessert that Daddy pushed back his chair. "I have something to talk over with all of you," he said. Eyes fastened on him questioningly. "This has been in the air for several weeks," he went on. "I haven't said anything before, because I hoped it would blow over. But we had a staff meeting at the office today and the thing looks pretty certain." He gazed around the table. "The head office is going to move to Pittsburgh."

Cathy's fork remained suspended. After a minute Chris said, "Do you have to go to Pittsburgh?"

"Won't you get the Promotion?" Cathy asked quickly.

"If I get the promotion," Daddy said slowly, "if I am made a vice-president, we shall have to go to Pittsburgh to live."

Chapter 6

Strangers

"Move out of this house?" Cathy cried. She could not believe she had heard her father right.

Daddy said, "Or I can keep my job as manager of the New York office, and we can stay here."

"Then we're going to stay here!" Cathy said fiercely. She loved this house passionately—her darling room where she could close the door and own the whole world, the living room with the fireplace, the attic, the gracious, curving stairway.

"Yes, we're going to stay!" Jeff echoed.

Mother threw them an understanding smile. "Daddy and I love this house too," she said. "We'd like to stay in Middle Bridge, even if it does mean giving up the promotion. The only thing is," Mother went on slowly, "we have spent a lot of money, because we counted on the promotion. And we need to spend a lot more to make the house what we want it. But if we stay here we won't have the extra income we counted on."

Three pairs of brown eyes rested on her anxiously. "I could pick berries next summer and sell them," Cathy said helpfully.

"I could do some jobs and get money," Jeff offered.

"Maybe we can find a buried trejur," Chris suggested.

63

"*Treasure*, Chris," Cathy said sharply.

"I have a suggestion," Mother said slowly, "but you would all have to co-operate."

"We will!" they shouted.

"Sure?" Mother looked at Cathy especially. Cathy nodded.

"Well, then," Mother said, "we could rent part of this house. We could make an apartment of the living room and TV room, with the laundry as a kitchen. The bathroom is right across the hall."

"But then we wouldn't have any fireplace for ourselves!" Cathy cried.

"It wouldn't be for always. Then upstairs . . ."

Cathy gave an exclamation of pain. "Not upstairs!"

"I'm just telling you what we could do," Mother pointed out. "In fact, Cathy, what we shall have to do for a while if we stay here. We can rent two rooms upstairs—yours and the guest room."

Cathy stared at her, unable to believe her ears. She turned despairingly to Daddy. "Do we have to?"

"We'll have to do something of the sort till we pay off these bills. There's the oil burner, and the new furniture, and the mortgage. Mother has figured out how many rooms we'll have to rent. Of course," her father reminded her, "we can go to Pittsburgh."

"But I don't want to go to Pittsburgh!" An aching lump swelled in Cathy's throat. "I want to stay here. I want to be the princess in the play. And there are the Brownies and junior choir and everything. Only I like this house the way it is—not with apartments and other people!"

"It would just be until we got caught up," Mother reminded her again.

Cathy could not accept it. "But why does my room have to be rented? Why can't Chris's be?"

"The rooms on your side of the hall are by themselves and they have the bathroom between them. They would be the logical ones to rent," Mother explained.

"But where would I sleep?"

"You can sleep in my room," Chris offered.

This was a new outrage and humiliation. "Do I have to sleep in her room?" Cathy demanded, her voice shaky.

"As I said before, we can move to Pittsburgh," Daddy repeated patiently.

"Can I have Jeffy's room?" Cathy asked.

"No!" Jeff shouted.

Mother leaned over and held Cathy's hand tightly for a moment. "We don't have to decide tonight," she said.

Cathy helped dry the dishes. Chris, who seemed rather pleased with this new idea that had turned up, chattered brightly. Mother seemed thoughtful, and Cathy put the dishes away and dried knives and forks in silence. The lump in her throat hurt, and a haze of tears made everything look blurry.

In spite of her anguish her mind was working feverishly. As soon as she had hung up the dish towel, she went upstairs and on up to the attic, snapping the light switch at the foot of the stairs. She looked around, shivering. Dismal and cold as the attic was, it would be better than going in with Chris!

"Mother," she said, going downstairs, "could I sleep in the attic?"

"In the attic! No, Cathy." Cathy turned away, her

mouth trembling. "Darling," Mother said, "would it be so awful to move in with your sister?"

Without speaking, Cathy ran upstairs. Move back with Chris? Never be by herself any more to read or dream or pretend? How could she bear it?

She closed her door, slipped out of her clothes,

and crept into bed. Something numb inside her would not let her cry—perhaps because she did not really believe this dreadful thing could happen. All she felt now was a need to get as far away from everyone as she could.

In the morning Cathy was no happier. Going to school with Chris, she faced a new problem. How can I tell the girls we have to rent rooms, after telling them all the things we were going to do, she thought. "I don't know what to say to all the kids about Daddy's not getting the Promotion," she said forlornly to Chris.

"Tell them we don't want to go to Pittsburgh, so we are going to take boarders," Chris said practically.

"Not boarders!" Cathy cried. "We are going to rent some apartments. I could say some people just begged us to let them come here."

"What people?" Chris asked.

"Oh, Chris, you don't understand anything!" Cathy cried. "Anyway, promise you won't tell anyone until I think what to say."

Cathy's mind was on the problem most of the morning. She had told the girls that she would invite them over soon. She had boasted about all the beautiful rooms and her own private suite. How could she tell them now that she and her family were only going to live in part of the house and let the rest?

During arithmetic she thought of the five little Peppers. The Peppers were very poor and lived in their kitchen all the time. Polly Pepper scrubbed the kitchen table until it was white. If we were very, very, very poor like the Peppers, I wouldn't mind, Cathy thought, because that would be fun. We could rent all our rooms except the kitchen. Mother could even get a job, and I could keep house and scrub the table.

The spirit of make-believe lifted Cathy out of her misery for a moment. Then she came out of her imagining. She was sure they were not as poor as that. She was just going to have to give up her private suite, and she couldn't bear it.

In the days that followed, it became understood that they were staying in Middle Bridge and renting rooms until they caught up on the bills. Cathy refused to discuss the subject, pretending to herself that nothing of the sort was about to happen.

Mother and Daddy were painting the extra bedroom in the evenings. "Perhaps you ought to move in with Chris now, dear," Mother told Cathy, "so we can get your room ready to rent."

They moved her on Saturday. In Cathy's heart there burned a fierce resentment. She did not offer to help move the furniture; she merely stood aside as Mother and Daddy moved the bed and Chris shoved furniture to make room.

"Well!" she announced, in the door of Chris's room. "If I have to be in here, the bookshelves and the bureaus are going to be in the middle of the room to make a wall!"

"Oh, Cathy, that would look terrible!" Mother exclaimed.

"I don't care. That's the way it's going to be."

"But I don't want it that way!" Chris was almost tearful.

"This is my room now as much as yours," Cathy informed her tartly. She knew she sounded mean and horrible, but she couldn't help it. There was a stinging, aching hurt inside her, and saying these unpleasant things seemed to ease the pain.

"Let's try it that way, Chris," Mother said quietly.

"We'll see how it works out." Chris made her little moaning sound of assent.

Cathy stalked to the door of Jeff's room. "Why can't Jeff move in with Chris?"

"I'd just as soon have Jeff," Chris said quickly. Cathy gathered that she would rather have him, under the circumstances. But Jeff, downstairs with his trucks, yelled, "No!" Cathy knew better than to press the issue.

The year was moving steadily toward spring. A wind like the deep roar of the sea still boomed in the pines, but tiny green and pink plants were pushing out of the ground. Often when Cathy came home from school, Mother was in the yard raking the dry leaves away from the flower beds. Whenever she uncovered the earth, tender, sturdy spears poked through. Cathy always dropped to her knees, talking softly to the little plants. "Oh, you darling babies," she murmured. "You are going to be lovely flowers soon." A spry little old man named Mr. Carmichael had come to plow up a patch of vegetable garden near the orchard.

Bicycles were parked outside the school now, and Cathy watched enviously as boys and girls mounted and rode off. "I wish I could have a bicycle," she said to Mother. It would help some, she thought, if she could only have a bicycle.

"All in good time," Mother told her.

Mother had put the studio couch in Cathy's room, with a chest of drawers and a comfortable chair. "If we rent the downstairs rooms unfurnished," she said, "we'll move some of that furniture up here."

Daddy put an ad in the New York Sunday papers as well as the local weeklies. "Gracious home in small village offers three-room unfurnished apartment," the ad said. "Fireplace. Victorian charm. Two furnished rooms also available."

He brought some replies home Monday night. Cathy would not admit that she was curious. She pretended to be buried in a book when Daddy read the letters after dinner.

"This one," he said, glancing at one of them, "is from an old lady who must have a house with no children in it."

"This is just the place for her not to come," Mother retorted.

"And this one is from an old gentleman."

"I refuse to run a nursing home," said Mother.

"Here is a woman who would like to open a beauty parlor."

Cathy looked up. It would be exciting to have a beauty parlor in the house. Maybe the lady would curl her hair for her and put polish on her nails. But Mother just gave Daddy a look.

Daddy picked up the next letter. "This one sounds promising. It is from a Mrs. Hughes. She says, 'My nine-year-old daughter and I are looking for a quiet, homelike apartment in a small town where she can be in school and I can have a spot in which to write without interruption. Perhaps your home would meet our need. Will you give us more particulars? We should like to come and see you.' She gives a New York phone," Daddy said, "and signs herself Alice Hughes."

Cathy was thinking, her eyes on her book but not seeing the page. A nine-year-old girl. How would it seem to have a girl her own age in the house? An upsurge of jealousy swept her. A girl living in this room, enjoying this fireplace, when she herself couldn't.

She gave a little grunt of anger and turned her back on the family. She knew Mother and Daddy both glanced in her direction, but she did not care.

"That's the best of the lot," Daddy said, gathering up the letters. "We'll probably have more tomorrow. Meanwhile, I'll call this Mrs. Hughes from the office."

On Tuesday Daddy reported to the family. "Mrs. Hughes is coming out Sunday afternoon to look the place over. And a young chap is coming Sunday morning to see the rooms upstairs. He might be willing to take both rooms."

Sunday was a mild day of hazy sunshine. Cathy was in the kitchen when the young man arrived in midmorning to look at the rooms. Resentful, yet curious in spite of herself and suddenly shy as well, she watched around the corner of the dining room as her mother led him upstairs. Chris and Jeff tagged along. He was a lean, cheerful-looking young man wearing a sports jacket.

Cathy got her coat and her soap-bubble set and went out on the side porch. She wanted to prove to herself and everyone else that she had become completely indifferent now as to who rented their rooms or whether anyone did. She took a good look at the prospective roomer's car, parked in the drive in front of the house. It was a good-looking sports model. Then she went back to the side porch and began to blow bubbles.

The fragile, rainbow-tinted balls drifted, lighter than air, toward the big tree that hid her secret pine house. Fairy balls, Cathy thought. Each one has a fairy inside. She blew another batch. I have to blow more balls before the others fall to the ground, or the fairies will die. The fairies lived in the pine house, she decided. They kept themselves warm with pine needles in winter. Now it was spring and the fairies would be throwing off their covers.

After a long time she heard voices and footsteps as the room-viewing party came downstairs. They stood at the open front door talking. Cathy kept on blowing bubbles. Then she heard the young man's voice as he went down the steps and Mother closed the door. The car spurted into life, appeared around the corner of the house, jogged easily over the hole in the drive, and disappeared down the road.

In a minute Chris came dashing out. "He's going to take both rooms!" she cried. "He likes them. He's going to move in next Sunday."

"So?" Cathy inquired rudely.

"So now we only have to rent the downstairs apartment. We like him—Jeff and me. He's nice. His name is Mr. Tracy."

"Well," Cathy said loudly, "I *don't* like him!" And suddenly, though a moment ago she had not thought of crying, Cathy dropped her bubble pipe to the ground, rushed into the house and upstairs, banged the door of the bedroom, and threw herself on her bed, sobbing. Deep in her heart she had hoped that no one would take her room. Now she had no place—no place! The storm pent up in Cathy broke loose in a torrent of sobs.

After a while she heard the door open softly, and Mother came in and sat down on the bed. Cathy sobbed harder. She felt like screaming and kicking and pounding the bed. She hated the new roomer who had taken her room away. But since he was coming, she was jealous of Chris and Jeff, who had seen and talked to him and were friends of his now, while she was an outsider. A fresh burst of heartbreak seized her.

"There now." Mother leaned over, put her arms around Cathy, and gathered her up. Cathy clung to her. Mother held her close. Then Cathy's sobs lessened and Mother began to talk, not about the room at all, but about all the lovely flowers they were going to have this spring, and the vegetable garden Cathy could plant herself. Cathy lay against her, shaken by the sobbing she could not stop, grateful not to discuss the whole hateful business.

"Come on," Mother said at last, "let's go outdoors, just you and I, and see what is coming up."

Chapter 7

Things Are Looking Up

The shower of tears seemed to clear the air. As Cathy and Mother wandered hand in hand through the yard, Mother discussing the best spot for Cathy to plant her garden, Cathy began to feel calmer, smoothed out. Deep inside she was ashamed, too, of the way she had acted, and she made a secret resolution never to behave like that again.

Still, as the time approached that afternoon for Mrs. Hughes and her daughter to arrive, Cathy was torn. She really wanted to co-operate now to make up for her outburst, yet try as she would she could not make herself act eager to have them come.

She was in the kitchen when the doorbell rang at about three o'clock. Mother, who had just finished the dinner dishes, slipped out of her apron to go to the door. Already Chris and Jeff could be heard pounding downstairs to inspect the callers.

"I'll be out in the yard," Cathy said hastily. Mother threw her a questioning look. "I'll come in in a few minutes," Cathy promised.

She went out and busied herself, getting down to brush the dead leaves from a flower bed. It was fascinating to clear away the damp leaves, smelling of

74

cold, musty earth, and find everywhere the new spears, so strong, so determined.

She had said she would go in. I must go now, Cathy thought, working away at the leaves, but resentment against these intruders was still fierce within her. After a while she heard Mother call, and she stood up with a feeling of relief that now she must go, whether she wanted to or not.

Mother and Mrs. Hughes and her daughter were sitting in the living room. Cathy took in the other girl in one quick glance—a slender, gray-eyed girl just her own height.

"Mrs. Hughes," Mother was saying, holding her hand out to Cathy with a smile, "this is my older daughter, Cathy. This is Mrs. Hughes, dear. And this is Naomi. They are coming to live with us. And what do you think? Mrs. Hughes writes books!"

"Oh!" Cathy said. She looked at Mrs. Hughes again with new interest. She added, a bit overcome at the thought of being in the presence of an author, "I love books!"

"Do you, Cathy?" Mrs. Hughes said.

Cathy stood awkwardly for a moment, then slid onto the stool beside her mother's chair, trying not to stare rudely at Mrs. Hughes. Mrs. Hughes's hair, dark and glossy, was bound in two braids around her head. Her eyes were gray, like her daughter's.

"Your mother tells me you are in the fourth grade," Mrs. Hughes said. "Naomi is too. It's nice that you are going to be classmates." She and Mother began to talk, and Cathy glanced shyly toward Naomi.

"What kind of books does your mother write?" she asked curiously.

"She writes girls' books," Naomi said. "For older girls."

"I like books about older girls," Cathy said quickly. "I like any kind of books."

"So do I," Naomi agreed.

"Are you going to bring the books with you?" Cathy demanded. Naomi nodded. "Oh, good!" Cathy felt a quickening of pleasure. "Can I read them? You can read my books if you'd like to."

Then she and Naomi were talking. She was telling Naomi her teacher's name and about school and how Jeff went to kindergarten on the school bus. Naomi seemed really interested, and the quick smile that lighted her face was friendly. Cathy warmed to her subject and described for Naomi with enthusiasm all the details of the play they were working on. "Maybe you can be in it too," she exclaimed, "if you come soon enough."

"I'd like to be," Naomi said.

By this time Mrs. Hughes and Mother had completed the arrangements, and Mrs. Hughes rose to go. Cathy was feeling better—much better. In fact, in this short half hour the future had taken on a different look. It might be very annoying to share her darling home with strangers, and moving in with Chris was still a bitter pill to swallow. But the advent of this friendly girl, Naomi, and her mother, who was a real live author, suddenly opened up new interest.

Daddy came in to meet Mrs. Hughes and Naomi. Chris and Jeff burst in from outdoors, panting and disheveled from play. "I'll let you know whether we can move our things on Saturday," Mrs. Hughes said. "I hope we can." She looked around at the five Leonards. "What a lovely family you have," she exclaimed to Mother. "I think we are very fortunate to be coming here, don't you, dear?" Naomi nodded and moved closer to her mother. Something in the movement was strangely touching to Cathy.

The taxi that had brought the Hugheses from the station was waiting. Cathy hopped up and down on the step as Naomi and her mother climbed into it. Her spirits were soaring now. She could hardly wait for Naomi to move in—for the novel experience of having another girl her own age living right in the house. It was going to be fun.

"Naomi!" she cried, running down to the side of

the taxi. "Come soon, so you can be in the play!" They all waved as the car drove off. Naomi's waving hand could still be seen as the taxi turned into the road and sped away.

Cathy's heart beat high and her cheeks were warm with excitement as she turned back toward the house. She caught her mother's smile. "I like Naomi!" she cried. "And I never thought an *author* would come here to live! Maybe she'll tell me how to write a book."

"We're fortunate to get such lovely people," Mother said.

All day Cathy had moped around. Now she felt in such high spirits that she had to let off steam. I will play I'm a lady, she thought, pausing in the hall. I have to rent a lot of rooms to support my twelve children. And I have to do all the work and everything.

She went upstairs and paused at the door of her room and Chris's, and the thought struck her that it looked just awful with the bookshelves and two bureaus lined up in the middle of the floor. I am going to change this room around, she decided impatiently. She went to the head of the stairs and called, "Chris! Come up and help me change our room around. It looks messy!"

Chris was pleased to come to her assistance. Daddy and Mother came too and shoved the bureaus against the walls, while Cathy took the bookshelves apart to move them. "There!" She surveyed the room with satisfaction when her parents had gone downstairs. "Play you're my little girl, Chris, and I'm your mother, and we have to sleep in the same room, because we're poor and all our other rooms are rented. And Jeff is my little boy and he has a cubbyhole in here." She glanced into Jeff's cubbyhole. "Mercy, I must pick up this boy's room!" she exclaimed, in disapproval of the trucks strewn on the floor.

Cathy's game carried over to suppertime. She was bursting with energy. "May I make some muffins?" she asked Mother, going busily into the kitchen. "Because I am a poor woman with twelve children." She made the muffins and bustled around setting the table. This was partly a game. It was partly, too, as if she felt driven to do everything she could to make up for her sulkiness and unpleasantness of the last few weeks. When she had wiped the dishes, still buoyed up by her new enthusiasm, she had another idea. "Mother," she said, "can I get up early and get Daddy's breakfast?"

"Why, I'd be delighted," Mother said. "It's awfully early, though. Daddy gets up before six."

"I can get up before six!" Cathy cried. "I'll set my alarm. And you don't even have to wake up."

"Very well, my pet," said Mother. "The pleasure is all yours. Then you'd better run right along and get some sleep."

On the other nights when she had shared Chris's room Cathy had gone to bed resentfully. Tonight she marched upstairs even before Chris and Jeff and got ready for bed in businesslike fashion. She turned the little alarm lever to "on" and set the clock on the floor beside her bed. Then she got into bed with a book.

Chris came up and Cathy closed her book, sliding down between the sheets. "Please go to bed quickly, Chrissy," she said, "and turn off the light. I'm going to get up very early to get Daddy's breakfast, but I won't wake you."

"O.K.," Chris said agreeably. Cathy snuggled down with a pleasant feeling of anticipation.

It was dark when the twang of the alarm finally penetrated her deep sleep. Mother had said six o'clock was early, so the darkness did not surprise her. It made the adventure much more exciting—almost like Christmas morning.

She got out of bed and turned off the alarm. Then she pulled on her clothes. She could, of course, just put on her bathrobe, but she was sure Polly Pepper was always neatly dressed when she got breakfast. She combed her hair, moving softly so as not to wake Chris, and even tiptoed when she went into the bathroom to wash her face and brush her teeth. I won't put on my shoes and stockings, though, she decided. It did feel so good to go barefoot, and Mother always objected when she did it.

Cathy went down, bare feet noiseless on the stair carpet, and pulled on the kitchen light with a cozy feeling that for this little time the place was hers. She tied on her apron. My, but she was still sleepy! Her eyes kept blinking so. She pressed the pilot button and lighted the gas range, ran water into the kettle, and set it to boil.

Daddy always ate breakfast in the kitchen. Cathy put eggs on to boil and poured orange juice. She set the table and got out bread and butter and the toaster.

He should be up by now, she thought suddenly. Maybe she should have waked him before she came down. Then she raised her head, listening. He was coming. Good, Cathy thought. Breakfast is all ready. She hastily measured a spoonful of instant coffee into the cup. A board creaked overhead, and in a minute she heard the padded sound of steps on the stairs.

Oh, the toast! She was just slipping two slices into the toaster when the door swung open and Daddy came in. She beamed at him.

"Good morning!" Cathy said, trying to sound bright. "Breakfast is all ready. I'll get the eggs now. You may sit right down," she added, as Daddy stood rubbing his tousled hair in a puzzled kind of way. Cathy noticed that he had on his bathrobe.

"What on earth!" Daddy said. "Do you know what time it is?"

"What time?" Cathy stood holding the saucepan with the boiled eggs in it.

"It's two-thirty!"

After one startled second Cathy gave a loud gasp and clapped a hand over her mouth. "I know what I did!" she exclaimed. "I turned on the alarm, but I forgot to set it!"

The toast popped into sight with a businesslike click. Suddenly Daddy gave a chuckle and Cathy began to giggle. She set the eggs down and threw herself against her father to muffle the sound. "No wonder I was sleepy," she gasped.

"Well, let's turn off the gas and go back to bed, Toots," her father suggested when they had had a good laugh. "At least breakfast is ready."

They went upstairs hand in hand and Daddy tucked her into bed once more. Cathy turned her face into the pillow to keep from waking Chris with her giggling. She was still shaking with smothered laughter about getting breakfast in the middle of the night as she dropped quickly off to sleep.

Chapter 8

Naomi Comes

"WHAT IS the girl's name?" asked Martha.

"Naomi," Cathy replied. "And her mother writes books. She is going to write books at our house. She might put us in a book, even!" This delightful thought had recently occurred to her. The group of girls in the schoolyard considered that aspect. They were more interested, however, in the new girl and what she was like.

The station wagon swooped up to the school walk and Bernice got out. The knot of girls was breaking up now to play a game, but Bernice caught up with Cathy. "How about coming over this afternoon?" she inquired.

Cathy had not yet visited at Bernice's. She shook her head now. "I can't. We're renting some apartments in our house and I have to help my mother."

"Renting apartments!" Bernice's eyes searched her face curiously.

"A girl and her mother are coming to live in three rooms on our first floor, and a man is going to have two rooms and a bathroom upstairs."

"Aren't you going to have that private suite?" Bernice demanded.

"Nope," Cathy said carelessly.

"Oh," Bernice said, and turned toward the game going on. The thought went through Cathy's mind, I'm glad she didn't get to be my best friend.

That afternoon after school Cathy helped shift furniture. Mr. Carmichael came in to help move the big pieces; the wiry little man lugged furniture upstairs while Mrs. Leonard hovered below, wearing a pained expression and murmuring worried protests. Cathy rushed around dragging chairs. Now that letting the rooms was no longer a troubled secret, now that the girls actually seemed to envy her having a new girl with an author-mother in the house, the whole affair had turned into an exciting adventure. Cathy was looking forward now to getting the rooms fixed up attractively for young Mr. Tracy and to seeing what Mrs. Hughes, and Naomi would do to the downstairs apartment when they arrived on Saturday.

She did glance into the bare living room regretfully. How she loved the fireplace! No more cozy reading before the fire while she toasted her bare toes. Cathy sighed. Even the game of being a poor woman with twelve children could not make up for that loss.

Saturday afternoon Cathy dashed through the house as the doorbell rang. Naomi stood at the door. Behind her in the driveway Cathy could see a shiny new blue car, from which Mrs. Hughes was removing an armful of clothes. Behind the car stood a moving van. Cathy forgot to ask Naomi in. "Is that your car?" she cried.

Naomi nodded happily. "We just bought it, because now we are going to live in the country."

Cathy remembered her manners. "Oh, come in," she cried, opening the door wide.

All afternoon the house was full of cold air and the heavy tramp of feet as movers unloaded the van and carried in furniture. Cathy was in the hall and in the Hughes's rooms until Mother said, "Cathy, you buzz around like a mosquito. Kindly come out and give these people a chance."

"She's not in the way," Mrs. Hughes said calmly. "Cathy, why don't you go over there with Naomi and help put books on the shelves?"

By suppertime Mrs. Hughes and Naomi were fairly well settled and the van had rumbled off down the drive. "What lovely old furniture!" Mother exclaimed. The rugs were beautiful too—Oriental, Mother said. There were two studio couches in the TV room and a chest of drawers and a big wardrobe to hold clothes.

What thrilled Cathy most was the grand piano. "Oh!" she gasped when it was carried in. "I always wished we had a piano!"

Mother went to get dinner while Cathy and Chris stood about watching Mrs. Hughes and Naomi put things into their drawers. Jeff, tiring of all this activity, had brought one of his trucks into the middle of the Hughes's living room. Mother came back.

"No trucks on this highway, my friend," she told her son, picking up the truck and taking him by the hand.

"I'll tell you what, Jeff." Mrs. Hughes sat down and drew Jeff toward her. "When I am not busy you may come and visit me sometimes. We'll read a story. Would you like that?" Jeff nodded. "We like little boys, don't we, Naomi?" Mrs. Hughes smiled at her daughter.

Naomi nodded, kneeling to give Jeff a quick hug. "You may come in whenever my mother isn't writing, Jeffy. You too, Chris." Cathy noticed Naomi's gentleness when she spoke to the children.

"Won't you and Naomi have supper with us?" Mrs. Leonard asked. But Mrs. Hughes said she and Naomi would christen their own little kitchen with a can of soup. "Then come along, Cathy," Mother said. "I need you to help me."

Back in the kitchen, she opened the oven door and lifted out a small pan of golden-brown, bubbling beans. "Take this carefully, Cathy," she said. "Tell Mrs. Hughes I baked these beans for them."

The next afternoon Mr. Tracy moved in. His belongings were loaded in his car, and Chris and Jeff were out of the house in a jiffy to help him carry things in. Cathy was shy; she had not met Mr. Tracy. She hovered near the top of the staircase until Mr. Tracy, passing her, said a friendly "Hi." She felt less strange then, but she did not rush out to his car like the other children; she wanted their roomer to realize that she was very grown-up, and not in their class at all.

"If those children bother you," she advised him loftily, as he came up the stairs laden and followed faithfully by his helpers, "I'll ask my mother to call them downstairs."

"Why, these two are the best assistants I've had in a month of Sundays!" Mr. Tracy exclaimed. Broad smiles spread across the faces of Chris and Jeff.

Cathy leaned against the door. Mr. Tracy seemed nice. "This is my room," she told him. "I mean, it used to be my room." She sighed. "And my private bath."

"We were going to have a guest room in that other

room," Chris explained. "Because Daddy was going to get a Promotion. Only he didn't get it."

"Chris, that's not right," Cathy exclaimed indignantly. "He could have had the Promotion, but we would have had to move to Pittsburgh. We didn't want to move to Pittsburgh; we wanted to stay here."

"So we have to take roomers," Chris added practically. "And you're one!" She poked her finger at Mr. Tracy.

"Don't be fresh, Chris," Cathy admonished in her most grown-up manner.

"We like roomers—nice roomers," she assured Mr. Tracy.

Mother called, and they went down reluctantly.

"Jeff, pick up your toys," Mother said. "Cathy and Chris, how about setting the table?"

Cathy was putting the knives and forks at the places when she noticed that Jeff had disappeared. That boy has gone up to Mr. Tracy's room, she thought. In a few minutes Chris said, "I have to get something upstairs." Cathy could stand it no longer. "Those children are upstairs bothering Mr. Tracy," she announced, going into the kitchen. "I guess I'll have to go call them."

As she went up the stairs she heard the soft strains of a stringed instrument. Mr. Tracy was seated in a chair, a guitar across his knees. Jeff leaned against him. Chris sat cross-legged on the floor. All three were engrossed, as Mr. Tracy sang softly to the sweet twang of the music, "She'll be comin' round the mountain when she comes . . ." Cathy was drawn into the room. She slid into a chair, sitting on the edge because it was piled with papers. In a moment she had forgotten she had come to get the children.

Then Mother appeared in the doorway, and the music stopped as Mr. Tracy looked up. "I didn't know we had rented a room to Pied Piper," Mother said, laughing. "I hate to interrupt that lovely music, but I have to feed these Indians, Mr. Tracy. I've set a place at the table for you."

Cathy skipped happily ahead. Jeff and Chris held tight to their new friend's hands as they all went downstairs together. There was a salad for supper and toasted crackers and cheese and cocoa and a fresh cake. Jeff beamed, because Mr. Tracy was sitting beside him, and hitched his chair closer. This is fun, Cathy thought. I like having roomers—I mean renting apartments—when such nice people come to live here.

Naomi was ready for school when Cathy knocked on the Hughes's door Monday morning. How pleasant and homelike the room looked! Cathy thought. The curtains were not up, but everything else seemed to be in place. The morning sun made it bright and cheerful. "Doesn't our house look nice?" Mrs. Hughes asked. Naomi looked happy, as she and her mother, Cathy, and Chris set out for school.

At recess, Cathy was proud to introduce Naomi to the other girls. Bernice, hovering on the edge of the circle surrounding the newcomer, seemed cool until Gretchen asked Naomi, "Where did you live before you came here?"

"In New York," Naomi said, "since we came back from Paris." Cathy looked at her in surprise. Neither Mrs. Hughes nor Naomi had mentioned living in Paris.

"Paris in Europe?" Gretchen's eyes were incredulous. Naomi nodded.

"That's in France," Martha added helpfully.

Bernice said nothing, but before they went back into the school, Cathy saw her sidle up to Naomi. "I have my own horse," she announced.

Naomi responded politely. "You have?"

"Can you ride?" Bernice wanted to know.

"I rode at camp last year."

"We can ride together sometimes," Bernice said. "None of these kids know how." Cathy was disturbed. Was Bernice trying to draw Naomi away, as she had tried at first to draw Cathy?

After school they told Naomi about the play. "Let's make a new character, so Naomi can be in it," Martha suggested.

"O.K.," Cathy cried. "What character would you like to be, Naomi? There's a princess—that's me—and a prince, and a king and queen, and a lot of pages and ladies in waiting. You could be the princess' sister."

"Or a fairy godmother," Gretchen cried.

"If you're a fairy godmother," Chris said, "you could change all the bad people to toadstools, Naomi."

"Toadstools!" Cathy cried. "Chris, why would she change people into toadstools?"

Chris looked doubtful. "Aren't toadstools those little animals that hop?"

"No!" Cathy cried, her laugh ringing out.

Everyone else laughed at Chris too—everyone but Naomi. Naomi spoke quickly. "You're thinking of toads, Chris," she said. "And I think it would be fun to be a fairy godmother and change all the bad people into toads!"

Naomi's tone quieted Cathy. "O.K.," she said, suddenly anxious to join Naomi in approving her sister. "And they can get down and hop around when they're changed. That's good, Chrissy!"

Later, Cathy heard Bernice say to Naomi, "When can you come over to my house to play?" She listened for Naomi's response, the disturbed feeling returning.

"I'll have to ask my mother," Naomi said. She slipped her arm into Cathy's. "I'd rather go home and play with you," she said softly, as they turned away. Cathy said nothing, but suddenly new respect was added to her liking for Naomi. She herself had not seen at first that Bernice was an unpleasant girl. Naomi had recognized it at once.

It was a damp, gray afternoon. The Hughes's door stood open as they all trooped into the front door and paused in the hall, and Cathy saw with delighted surprise that a brisk fire was burning in the fireplace. "Oh," she cried, "a fire!" and started toward it. Then she stopped, stricken, and looked at Mrs. Hughes. "I forgot I'm not supposed to come in here!"

"Of course you are." Mrs. Hughes smiled at her. "You're coming in to share our fire, I hope."

"Oh, thank you!" Cathy walked slowly over to the piano. She fingered the keys lightly. "We were going

92

to get a piano," she said regretfully, "but I guess we can't right now. I was going to take music lessons."

"Naomi is going to have lessons," Naomi's mother said, "if we find a good teacher. Perhaps you could have lessons on this piano."

Cathy faced her, hardly able to believe her ears. "Oh, I want to tell Mother!" She rushed upstairs. "Mother, Mrs. Hughes says I can have music lessons on her piano! Can I, Mother, can I?"

"That is very nice of Mrs. Hughes," Mother declared. "Perhaps it can be arranged, dear."

Cathy was so exuberant that she had to go outdoors to let off steam. "Come on, Naomi," she begged. "I'll show you the town."

She led the way across the street and between the houses to South Street. Two dogs came galloping to meet them. "Hi, Beans. Hello, Custer." She patted their heads. "They all know me," she explained to Naomi. Naomi stopped to stroke their heads and they lifted friendly eyes to her face.

"The store's across the street," Cathy pointed out. "I'll take you in and introduce you to Mrs. Himmel." She opened the door briskly. "Hello, Mrs. Himmel. This is Naomi. She lives at my house now. In case she comes in to buy something, you'll know who she is."

"Glad to meet you, Naomi," Mrs. Himmel said, her heavy face beaming. "You come in any time."

It was fun to be introducing Naomi to Middle Bridge. Cathy felt as if she herself had lived here always. "And this is the post office." She led her into the other building. "Hi, Mrs. Baker. This is Naomi Hughes. If she gets any mail, you can put it in our box."

Cathy took Naomi down South Street as far as

the bridge. Beyond it the road curved out of sight through the woods. They leaned over the rail, watching the small stream of water going over the dam. Then they cut back to North Street and turned toward home.

"This is the pine house," Cathy said, as they went through the yard. She pointed to the low branches. "It's my secret house. The fairies live there. Sometimes I send the fairies home in bubbles." They went on around the back of the house and peered into the darkness of the barn.

Cathy showed her companion the garden patch. "Chris is going to have a garden too, and so is Jeff." She paused. "Would you like to have a garden?" Naomi nodded. "Let's go ask Mother." Cathy was off at top speed, Naomi following. "Mother!" Cathy shrieked, bursting in at the back door. "Can Naomi have a garden too, like us kids?"

"If she would like one." Mother smiled at their eagerness.

"She would; wouldn't you, Naomi?"

"Yes! I never had a garden." Naomi's cheeks were flushed, her eyes sparkling.

"Come on out again," Cathy cried joyfully. "I want to show you where all the flowers are growing."

The dry leaves were all off the little plants now, and the tender green stalks were growing boldy. Naomi knelt and examined them with shining eyes. "Oh, it's going to be so pretty here!" she cried, standing up and gazing about her. "It's going to be as pretty as Paris in the spring!"

Cathy looked at her respectfully. "Why did you live in Paris?"

"My father worked for the United Nations," Naomi explained. "He died two years ago."

"Oh." Cathy felt a strange sense of shock at the thought of a father dying. "Did you come back then?"

"We stayed there for a while. Then we came back to New York and lived with my aunt. But Mother couldn't write there, so we moved to an apartment hotel, until we saw the ad about your house." Naomi gave a long sigh and gazed around the garden.

Standing there looking at her—this other girl who longed for a real home—Cathy felt a sensation she had never known before. Suddenly the safety and sweetness of her own family lay around her like a warm cloak. She put her arm around Naomi impulsively. "Well, I'm glad you saw that ad," she said gently.

With their arms around one another, they went into the house together.

CHAPTER 9

The Brownie Party

"HAVE YOU ever been a Brownie?"
Cathy asked Naomi. Mrs. Hughes was
out, and the girls had been doing long
division in front of the fire this raw,

rainy afternoon. Now they lay side by side on their
stomachs in front of the blinking coals, their bare feet
in the air and their dolls propped beside them.

"No, but I always wanted to be," Naomi said. "We
didn't stay any place long enough in New York."

"Well, you can be one here," Cathy assured her.
"All the girls are Brownies."

She heard Chris and Jeff burst into the back door. In a minute they were charging into Naomi's living room, wet and bedraggled.

"You two come in here and play," Mother called from the library, but Naomi sat up. "They may come in," she said quickly. "Come here, Jeffy, I'll help you take off your coat." Naomi was always so nice to the children that somehow it placed a new value on Chris and Jeff. Cathy often found herself looking at her brother and sister with new eyes these days.

"Mother." With distress in her voice Chris trotted across the hall to where her mother sat mending. "I

just realized something."

"What did you just realize?" Mother inquired.

"I just realized that my birthday comes on Brownie meeting day. And I wanted to have a party! But nobody could come to my party. I couldn't come to my party, either!" she added with a worried little giggle.

"That problem is easily solved," Mother assured her. "You ask Mrs. Lacy if you may have the Brownie meeting here."

"O.K.!" Chris sounded relieved. "Can we have a birthday cake and ice cream?"

"I shouldn't wonder."

Chris skipped happily into the hall. "Oh, goody, goody! Jeffy," she called, "let's go up in the attic and look for buried trejur."

Naomi and Cathy exchanged a smile of understanding at Chris's happiness. For once Cathy did not feel compelled to correct her sister's pronunciation.

The two girls went on talking. There seemed to be no end to the things they had to discuss. Now and then the fire popped and glowed brightly for a moment. Across the hall Cathy was aware of Mother by the window. There was no sound from Chris and Jeff in the attic.

After a while the children could be heard clumping downstairs, chattering to one another. They came on down to the first floor, and Chris trotted in to Mother once more.

"Mother," Cathy heard her say in a worried tone, "there's something in the attic. I think it's a skeleton." Cathy's eyes widened and she and Naomi looked at one another.

"Oh, no, dear!" Mother said quickly.

"It's just like a skeleton," Chris persisted. "It has bare bones."

Even in the cheerful warmth from the fire Cathy felt her flesh creep. "Where is it?" Mother asked.

"Way, way back where it's dark. Jeffy and me were looking for buried trejur."

Cathy had never explored those shadowy regions.

Now, hearing Chris's description of bare bones, she did not find it hard to believe that awful things lay hidden there. She gave a long delicious shiver and moved closer to Naomi.

"Come on up and look," Chris said.

Cathy and Naomi huddled together, giggling softly. "All right," Mother said boldly. "We will. Come on!"

"Let's go too!" Naomi whispered. Cathy scrambled to her feet and they followed Mother and Chris, Jeff trotting after them.

"I'll show you just where it is," Chris was saying importantly, leading the way up the second flight. She went briskly across the attic. Cathy and Naomi hung back, clutching one another.

Chris trotted right into a black alcove behind a chimney, and such delicious thrills chased up and down Cathy's spine that she moaned, "O-oh!" and backed toward the stairs.

Mother moved closer to the shadows. Cathy gave a loud squeal at what they might see and ran part way downstairs, peering fearfully up over the stair rail, ready to flee.

Suddenly Mother laughed out loud. "That's not a skeleton, Chris! It's an old dressmaker's dummy." She reached in and dragged a curious figure toward the light, while Cathy came bravely back. "See, it's a frame the shape of a lady. Women used to get one in their own size to fit clothes on when they sewed."

"Well, it looked like a skeleton!" Chris was somewhat taken back. And now Cathy and Naomi, weak with relief, were hugging one another and laughing hysterically. They were all laughing, even Chris.

"I see why you thought it was a skeleton, Chris,"

Naomi cried, examining the dummy. "It's just the shape of a person, without a head, and those wire things do look like ribs."

"We can dress her up, Chris." Cathy looked over the buxom figure approvingly. "She can be the lady who's in charge of this tower."

"See, it's a good thing you found her," Naomi said.

"And you were very brave to go into that dark corner," Cathy added quickly.

"Hello, Mrs. Lady," Jeff said, patting the figure affectionately.

So Chris was pleased with herself after all, they had a new plaything, and they all trooped down to tell Naomi's mother, who had just come in, about the skeleton in the attic.

There was great excitement on Brownie meeting day as all the Brownies from Middle Bridge School went thronging to Mrs. Lacy's to wait for the Chestnut Hollow contingent before continuing on to Chris's party. Cathy took Naomi in charge, introducing her to Mrs. Lacy.

The bus arrived at last and a second band of brown-clad elves disembarked to join their fellow Brownies. "I think we're all here now," Mrs. Lacy said. "Those of you who have bicycles go on ahead. Who wants to walk and who wants to go in my car? Mike," she instructed her own five-year-old son, "you go get in the car now."

Chris climbed into the car. Cathy and Naomi elected to walk with Martha and Gretchen.

When they burst through the front door of the Leonard house, Cathy saw that Naomi's door was open. In fact, the Brownies who had arrived first were already swarming into the Hughes's apartment. She quickly looked a question at her mother as she came in from the kitchen. "It's all right," Mother assured her. "Mrs. Hughes suggested you have your meeting in there, because the room is larger."

How nice, Cathy thought, pleased to have the whole house opened up as if just one family lived here. The girls left their coats in the TV room. "Come on, Mike," Cathy said, taking the little boy's hand. "Let's go find Jeff. Jeff!" she shouted. "Here's someone to play with you."

Jeff appeared at the top of the stairs. "You go on up with Jeff. He'll let you play with his trucks," Cathy said, and Mike ascended without urging.

Brownies were swarming all over the first floor now. "Cathy, go and get them," Mrs. Lacy pleaded. Between them Naomi and Cathy rounded up the strays, and Mrs. Lacy called the meeting to order.

"Who is in the color guard?" she asked. "Me," Cathy said promptly, jumping up. She and three other Brownies stood in line. Gretchen held the flags as the guard advanced and the salute was given.

"Now," Mrs. Lacy said, "we'll have our election of officers. Nominations for president are in order."

A hand shot up. "Do you want to nominate someone?" Mrs. Lacy asked. The girl, who was from Chestnut Hollow School, nodded. "Who is it?" Mrs. Lacy asked.

"Me."

There was a general stir and giggle and Mrs. Lacy said quickly, "We don't nominate ourselves, dear. We leave that to someone else. Who has a nomination to offer?"

Cathy was thinking, I would like to be the president. I would like to stand up in front and preside. For some reason she imagined herself presiding not in a Brownie dress, socks, and stubby shoes, but in her trailing dress-up gown and, naturally, the silver slippers. She came back to reality as she heard Martha say, "I nominate Cathy."

"I nominate Naomi," Bernice said quickly.

"Cathy and Naomi leave the room, please, while we vote," Mrs. Lacy said.

Naomi protested. "I'm too new!" But Cathy saw the expression of pleased surprise in her eyes. And suddenly, as they left the room together, for some reason that she did not wholly understand she leaned over and whispered to Martha, "Vote for Naomi!"

She and Naomi stood in the dining room, waiting to be called back. "Cathy, I hope they elect you." "I hope they elect you," Cathy repeated stoutly.

Whether it was because she had whispered to Martha or because Naomi was the newest member, Cathy did not know; but Naomi was elected. Mrs. Lacy called her to come up front and preside. Cathy could not help feeling a few twinges of envy. I did want to be the president, she thought wistfully.

Martha was named treasurer, and with this important business out of the way the Brownies broke out of bounds again. One small girl from Chestnut Hollow gazed around the hall. "Whose house is this— yours or Naomi's?" she inquired of Cathy. Cathy started to say, "Mine." Then she glanced toward Naomi. "And Naomi's—and Chris's too, of course," she added. A quick flush of pleasure rose in Naomi's cheeks.

Cathy went into the kitchen now to tell Mother they were ready for the party. Chris was too excited to go. Mother had lengthened the dining-room table.

102

Each place was set with a gaily colored napkin, a glass of punch, and a small paper cup of candies. At each place was a white-iced cupcake bearing a birthday candle. Mother went around the table lighting the candles. "Bring in the ice cream," she told Cathy, and Cathy carried in the paper plates.

Gathered around the table, they sang "Happy birthday, dear Chris!" and Chris's brown eyes shone in the candlelight. "Let's all blow out our candles," Martha cried.

"Wish, Chris!" Naomi said quickly. "Make a good wish." Chris thought for a long moment, head on one side. Then she nodded, and the candles went out in a haze of smoke and a smell of burning wax. The Brownies tackled their refreshments with a will.

They were buzzing so happily together that no one noticed the stealthy creaking of the stairs around the corner in the hall. Cathy was seated at the end of the table toward the library. Suddenly she and all the other Brownies jumped as two masked bandits with guns pounced into the room screaming shrilly at the top of their lungs. "Bang, bang, bang!"

"Jeff!" Cathy cried, helpless with laughter after the sudden shock, as the Brownies squealed their protest at this surprise attack.

"Bang, bang, bang!" yelled the bandits again. But, tickled to death at surprising so many intended victims at one swoop, they shot no one. Instead, they slid quickly into chairs which had been set for them and proceeded to gobble their ice cream.

Chris hasn't opened her presents, Cathy remembered suddenly. She slipped out of her chair and went into the Hughes's living room to gather the packages some of the girls had brought.

Chris deserted her ice cream to open them. There was material for doll dresses, a white blouse, an Easter egg. Naomi had given her a book. Chris unwrapped a Brownie pencil, a pocketbook. Most exciting of all, to judge by the look on Chris's face, was a nurse's kit. Chris lifted out the thermometer and stethoscope, examining everything with an expression of delight.

Naomi spoke softly into Cathy's ear. "Let's play we're hurt so she can come and give us first aid."

Once Cathy might have pretended to be bored with that idea. Now she collapsed on the floor. "Help!" she moaned. "Those bandits wounded me. Nurse, come help me!"

"Come help me, too," Naomi cried, falling beside her. The nurse responded promptly, sticking a pretend needle into each of her patients.

All the other Brownies suddenly became first-aid cases, lying limply about the floor as if strewn there by some gigantic catastrophe. All lay seemingly lifeless as the nurse, cap askew on her head, pretend glasses on nose and needle in hand, went happily about, administering aid and comfort.

At last it was time for the party to end. The girls began to struggle into their coats. They thanked Chris for the party, and departed, singly and in pairs and groups, on bicycles, afoot, and in family cars. Cathy stood on the steps waving them all off. Chris blissfully applied first aid to Jeff, a willing patient.

They were all gone at last. Jeff, fully recovered from whatever ailed him, had come out and was shooting after Mrs. Lacy's car while Mike, kneeling at the rear window, returned the fire. Chris had gone off to gather up her presents and gloat over them.

"Come on in, Jeff, you'll catch cold," Naomi said in motherly fashion, putting her arms around Jeff's plump stomach and lugging him indoors.

Then Naomi went straight to her mother. "They elected me president!" she said, wonder in her voice. She threw her arms around her mother and laid her head against her. As she released herself and stood upright she exclaimed, "I'm so *glad* we live here! It's just like having real sisters and a real little brother. I hope we can live here forever!"

Smiling to herself, Cathy went off to help her mother clear the party table. In the library Chris was fussing happily over her presents. Cathy passed her with a benevolent glance of understanding, and did not suggest that she might help. She heard Mr. Tracy come in and Chris call to him excitedly, but she did not turn back. This was Chris's day—Chris's and Naomi's.

Something inside her was soaring on wings as she piled the paper plates and collected cups. I'm glad Naomi was elected instead of me, she thought, the dark cloud of envy all swept away. Because it makes Naomi so happy!

CHAPTER 10

Spring

SPRING PASSED through Middle Bridge in a pageant of changing color and bloom. First the daffodils, like rows of dancers in yellow skirts, swayed to the wind's music. Fragrant blue and pink and white hyacinths enchanted Cathy, who had never seen them before outside a florist's pot. All day and through the long dusk the forsythia bushes burned with a golden flame. Now the branches of the peach trees were lined with tight pink buds.

Cathy, coming home one day across the back yards with Naomi and Martha, dropped to the ground and threw her books aside. "Look!" she cried. Deep in the grass stood a tiny fluted trumpet of a flower—white, striped with palest pink.

"That's a spring beauty," Martha said. "They grow everywhere in the grass. I think they're all over your yard."

In a few days the Leonard lawn was a meadow of spring beauties. Cherry blossoms burst into flower like fluffy popcorn. The gnarled apple trees in the orchard opened their exquisite blooms of palest pink. Cathy, running into the orchard one day, suddenly stood still at the sight of tall, sturdy, big-petaled blue violets in the deep grass at her feet. She drew a

breath of wonder and gazed about her.
Violets were everywhere—purple, white,
yellow, blue—in reckless, riotous profusion.
Under one of the flowering apple trees a
carpet of violets spread like deep blue velvet beneath the shell-pink blossoms.

"O-oh!" Cathy breathed. She dropped to
her knees and began to pick. Here was
something she had dreamed of—all the
flowers she wanted and more, all at once,

for her hands to hold and her eyes to feast on. She stood up and let her eyes travel over the magic carpet.

"It's just like Heidi and the Alpine meadows," she breathed out loud. "I'm going to tell Chris and Mother and Naomi!" But she lingered, feasting on this secret storehouse of wonder for a while.

Now, on her way home from school, Cathy often stood still to hear a rushing sound that was not the wind in the treetops. It was water going over the falls. Sometimes after school she and Naomi walked down to the bridge, to hang over the railing and watch the foaming water rush over the dam. A mist drifted up, damp and cold. In the black, still night the hurrying brook sent a lullaby through Cathy's open window.

By midafternoon the peepers were piping away down by the water, their silvery chorus jingling across the town. When Cathy hung over the falls, the peeper song mingled with the rush of water, sounding so close that she felt she should be able to see one of the singers. A peeper seemed mysterious to her—a ghostly being that hardly existed save for the melody it made.

Flowering quince and a Judas tree flamed in front of the house. Then the purple and white lilacs were in blossom, holding their plumed spears high above Cathy's reaching hands. Mother cut great bunches, and Cathy buried her face in their elusive fragrance. The wisteria vine blossomed on the side porch and bees hummed all day in the heavy lavender clusters.

In Cathy's and Naomi's gardens peas and scallions were growing. When they drove over back roads to shop in Springdale, they saw farmers busy on the clean-plowed earth of their rolling fields and new lambs gamboling in the meadows.

The girls gave their play for the P.T.A. meeting. All the mothers and some of the fathers, including Mr. Leonard, were there. Cathy was so radiantly happy in her princess robes that she forgot to be nervous. Chris was a sweet lady in waiting, her silver cap slipping from her fair hair. Naomi, as the fairy godmother, turned the wicked people into toads that hopped to their doom, while the princess and prince reigned triumphant. Afterward there was coffee and cake for the grownups, and cold drinks for thirsty and excited actresses.

Cathy went home in a dream and drifted around the bedroom, still a princess, until Mother firmly tucked her into bed and turned out the light.

Cathy and Naomi raced home from school the day after the play. The music teacher was coming this afternoon and Cathy was to have her first lesson.

"You take your lesson first," Naomi said. "I'll go outdoors and Mother is out, so we won't make you nervous."

Cathy waited and watched for the teacher with racing heart. She was going to learn to play some pieces! This was almost as wonderful, as magical, as an orchard full of flowers.

She loved Miss Martin within ten minutes after her arrival. They sat down together at the piano and Miss Martin opened the yellow songbook that would unlock secrets for Cathy. Finally Miss Martin said, "There now, that's good. You practice each of these little songs five times every day and we'll see how well you can do them by next week."

Cathy took the book and ran to her mother, breathless, her pulse racing. "I really played them all!" she cried. "It wasn't very good, of course. But I'm going to practice them a million times, every day! And I'll teach you, too, Chrissy," she promised loyally, as her sister gazed in admiration.

So spring moved into dogwood time, and white petals tipped the green woods on the nearby hills like a fall of snow.

It was on a lovely, mild May evening that Daddy arrived home a little earlier than usual and came through the house into the kitchen. Cathy was making muffins and Chris, somewhat smeared, was stirring up gingerbread for dessert.

"Well, hello!" Mother said, giving him a kiss. "You look like the cat who's just eaten a mouse. What's happened?"

Daddy laid his evening paper on the table. "What's happened?" he repeated. Although he tried to sound casual, there was a note of suppressed excitement in his voice that made Cathy look up. "Well, several things." Cathy stood with a spoonful of batter in her hand. Chris, licking the gingerbread bowl, turned a smeared face toward her father.

"We had a meeting at the office today," Daddy said. "The plans are changed."

"What plans?" Cathy demanded.

"The head office is not going to Pittsburgh after all."

They stared for a moment, unable to comprehend. Finally Chris said, "Then will you get the Promotion?"

"Yes!" Daddy said, in a loud, happy voice.

Chris jumped up and down, and suddenly the full meaning broke over Cathy. If Daddy got the Promotion, that meant they would not need to rent part of the house—they could have it all to themselves as they had expected to have it in the first place. They could do all the things they had planned to do. They could buy a piano!

But that meant . . . She said quickly, "Has Naomi got to move?"

"It seems too bad," Mother said slowly, "just when they're settled so nicely and Naomi is enjoying school and everything so much. But I know you children can't wait to get those rooms—and the fireplace—back."

"She loves it here!" Cathy said. "She wants to live here forever. She said so. And she's Brownie president. And her garden is just growing." Suddenly her own passionate love of Middle Bridge and her home here gave Cathy insight into what it would mean to Naomi to leave it all: to leave this house where so much love and friendly laughter reached out to shelter her, too. In the space of a breath, Cathy weighed her own desires against Naomi's need. "Oh, Daddy, please, please don't make Naomi move away!"

Daddy looked down at her with an odd expression. "I guess that's up to you girls," he said. "How about Mr. Tracy?"

"He can stay until he finds another place that he likes," Mother said. "Can't he, Cathy?"

Cathy nodded. "I'm in no hurry. I don't mind sleeping in Chris's room." But as she thought about having her room back—her own darling room—her excitement mounted.

"Can I tell Naomi?" she cried. Mother nodded. "You finish the muffins," Cathy said, thrusting the spoon into her mother's hand. "Please." She ran into the other room, Chris at her heels, and knocked on Naomi's door.

"Come in," Mrs. Hughes's voice called from the kitchen. Naomi was sitting in the big chair, reading.

112

"Naomi," Cathy cried, "guess what!" Naomi looked at her expectantly. "The main office—my daddy's main office—isn't going to move to Pittsburgh! And my daddy is going to get the Promotion after all!"

In her excitement she had not thought of what Naomi's reaction might be. Now, as Naomi stared in surprise, the healthy outdoor color drained slowly from her face. Cathy realized, suddenly, what she was thinking. "But you can stay!" she cried. "We want you to stay anyway, Naomi. We've got plenty of rooms."

"O-o-oh!" Naomi let out a long-drawn sigh as the pink rushed back to her cheeks.

Mrs. Hughes had heard. She came into the room and sat down on the arm of Naomi's chair. "I'm so glad for your daddy and all of you," she said. "And we're glad we can stay, aren't we, Naomi? Some day"—she glanced down at her daughter—"we may find a little house for ourselves that we will love."

Naomi glanced up. "In Middle Bridge?" "Yes," said her mother. "With a garden," Naomi added. "With a garden," her mother said.

"Well, you don't have to hurry, anyhow," Cathy told them with a happy sigh.

Dinner was a gay event. "Hey, I just thought of something!" Cathy cried, pausing as she buttered her baked potato. "I'll be able to invite Judy soon." She had almost forgotten her friend in the city and her dream of entertaining her in the guest room.

She paused as another thought struck her. "Chris," she said, turning to face her sister, "if you would like to have the guest room for your bedroom, we could use your room for the guest room."

The light that broke over Chris's face was her reward. "Cathy! Honest?"

Cathy looked at her mother. "Is it all right?" Mother nodded, her smile like a warm embrace.

"Cathy," Chris said earnestly, "I won't go into your room when you don't want me to."

"Thank you, Chrissy," Cathy said. A quick, unaccustomed bond of warmth rushed between them.

They were eating gingerbread and whipped cream when Daddy said, "I almost forgot. I stopped in Springdale before I came home, and guess what I brought." They eyed him expectantly; this was a day of surprises. "I bought a bicycle, for one thing," Daddy said.

"Daddy!" Cathy almost shouted in her excitement. "For me?"

"Who else? And I bought two scooters. They'll be out in a day or so." Chris and Jeffy clapped loudly. "For the lady of the house"—Daddy grinned at Mother—"I bought the biggest, reddest pocketbook I could find!"

The bicycle was there a few days later when Cathy came home from school. She could not wait to try it. Mother came out to hold it for her while she rode up and down the drive. Down the drive they went. Dismount. Turn the bike. Up the drive. Then Mother got on and rode it herself, her pink cheeks making her look especially pretty.

"This time I bet I can do it!" Cathy climbed hopefully on once more as Mother held seat and handle bars. "You let go," she cried, as she mounted unsteadily to the seat and her feet moved the pedals. Mother took her hand from the bars but kept her grip on the seat. "Please let go!" Cathy begged breathlessly.

Mother let go. But the wheel was rolling downhill at a faster speed than Cathy could control. She wobbled. She tried valiantly to regain her balance. Then the front wheel turned sharply to one side, the bicycle tipped, and Cathy was on the ground in a disheveled heap.

Mother was there in an instant to help her and pick up the bicycle. "Now you're really learning to ride," she assured her, as Cathy brushed herself off and examined a skinned knee. "Nobody ever becomes a bicycle rider without a few tumbles."

"Cathy!" Chris was galloping down the drive. "I'll get my nurse's kit. Wait for me!"

Cathy waited, glad of an excuse for delay before she mounted the bicycle again. Chris brought the kit, set it down in a businesslike way, and applied a band-aid to the scraped knee. "There," she said with satisfaction. "Isn't that good?"

"It's fine. Thank you," Cathy said. Now she was ready to start again. "Get out of my way, everybody! But you'd better hold on this time," she added to Mother with a giggle. She was warm and perspiring, and her knee smarted, but she was supremely happy. "I'll teach you to ride, Chrissy," she said breathlessly, when she stopped to rest.

Daddy helped her practice on Sunday, and by Sunday night Cathy found that she could ride by herself. The trick of balancing, so baffling at first, was suddenly a simple matter.

"Oh, Daddy, can I go down the road a ways?" she cried.

"Get off your bike if you hear a car coming," Daddy said.

She rode, not wobbling too much, down the road as far as the bridge, the breeze soft against her face. How wonderful it was to have a bicycle to carry her so swiftly! Like a magic carpet sailing through space. She stopped at the bridge to rest, leaning over to watch the foaming rush of white water in the dusk and listen to the full, loud chorus of the peeper song all around her.

Then reluctantly Cathy turned and started back. She was tired now. She dismounted and slowly walked her bicycle up the drive through the fragrant twilight. Passing the pine tree, she stopped to rest for a minute, gazing into its shadowy branches. The fairies are home for the night in the pine-tree house, she thought. "Good night, fairies dear," Cathy said softly.

Daddy stood waiting at the front steps. The house loomed huge and ghostly white behind him, its windows beacons of brightness in the dusk. Mother was probably starting to get supper now, for the kitchen windows were alight. The children were playing in the library. I'll read a story to them before supper, Cathy thought. And over on their side, Naomi and her mother were having a quiet time together.

In the big house, everyone was home for the night.